Dvořák

in America

Dvořák

in America

In Search of the New World

Joseph Horowitz

Cricket Books
A Marcato Book
Chicago

Library of Congress Cataloging-in-Publication Data

Horowitz, Joseph, 1948–
  Dvořák in America : in search of the New World / Joseph
Horowitz.— 1st ed.
    p. cm.
"A Marcato book."
Summary: An account of Antonín Dvořák's 1890s stay in America,
where he took the essences of Indian drums, slave spirituals, and
other musical forms and created from them a distinctly new music.
Includes bibliographical references and index.
  ISBN 0-8126-2681-8 (cloth : alk. paper) — ISBN 0-8126-2692-3 (paper :
alk. paper)
  1. Dvořák, Antonín, 1841–1904—Journeys—United States—Juvenile
literature. 2. United States—Description and travel—Juvenile
literature. 3. Composers—United States—Biography—Juvenile
literature. [1. Dvořák, Antonín, 1841–1904. 2. Composers.
3. Music—United States—History and criticism. 4. United
States—Description and travel.] I. Title.
  ML3930.D9 H67 2003
  780'.92—dc21

                                                      2002151456

For Bernie and Maggie

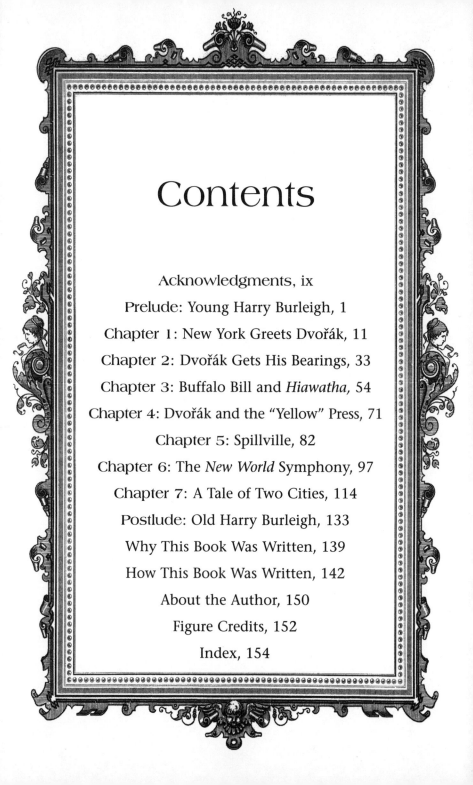

Contents

Acknowledgments, ix

Prelude: Young Harry Burleigh, 1

Chapter 1: New York Greets Dvořák, 11

Chapter 2: Dvořák Gets His Bearings, 33

Chapter 3: Buffalo Bill and *Hiawatha*, 54

Chapter 4: Dvořák and the "Yellow" Press, 71

Chapter 5: Spillville, 82

Chapter 6: The *New World* Symphony, 97

Chapter 7: A Tale of Two Cities, 114

Postlude: Old Harry Burleigh, 133

Why This Book Was Written, 139

How This Book Was Written, 142

About the Author, 150

Figure Credits, 152

Index, 154

Acknowledgments

In 2001, with the support of the American Symphony Orchestra League, I was able to secure an education grant from the National Endowment for the Humanities (which requires that I state that "any views, findings, conclusions, or recommendations" here expressed "do not necessarily represent those of the NEH"). This book is one result. Another is an extraordinary DVD created by Robert Winter and Peter Bogdanoff, *From the New World: A Celebrated Composer's American Odyssey.* Their interactive program includes all the music pertinent to chapters 5 and 6, including the *New World* Symphony, the *American* String Quartet, and the *American* Suite. In addition, Dvořák's visit is documented in contemporaneous newspapers and magazines. This material, and much else (including lesson plans and tips on how to read music), is organized to facilitate cross reference with my narrative.

I have long shared my obsession with Dvořák in America with Robert Winter and with the Dvořák scholar Michael Beckerman, both of whom offered generous feedback as I developed my manuscript. Charles Olton, president of the American Symphony Orchestra League, was a crucial supporter. At the New England Conservatory, then-president Robert Freeman, and Larry Scripp and Greg Gatien of the Music in Education Department, from the first understood what I was attempting and what I needed in order to achieve it. The same was true of Ron Gwiazda and Chuck Aversa at the Boston Latin School. I am also grateful to Larry Tamburri and others at the New Jersey Symphony, and to David Beauchesne and David Myers at George State University, for their participation in testing and evaluating the larger National Endowment for the Humanities project, and to William Zambelli of the American Symphony Orchestra League for his help in administering the grant. Others whose advice I relied upon included the Harry Burleigh scholar Jean Snyder, my agent Elizabeth Kaplan, and my editors—Marc Aronson and Carol Saller. My wife Agnes and daughter Maggie endured my absorption in this as in other book projects. My son Bernie, being fifteen, was the project guinea pig.

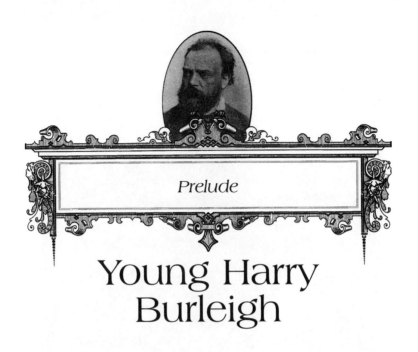

Young Harry Burleigh

Harry Burleigh shinnied up the lamp pole. Clinging with his legs, he filled the cup with kerosene oil and lit the wick with a match. The lamp emitted a soft glow, illuminating the docks and railroad tracks, freighters and passenger steamers of the Erie, Pennsylvania, lakefront. Harry's grandfather, Hamilton Waters, was the official lamplighter. But Hamilton was nearly blind, so his grandsons Harry and Reginald helped out, accompanying him on his rounds every evening at dusk.

They didn't mind the work because they enjoyed the company. Born to slavery in Maryland, Hamilton Waters had led a hard, eventful, and fulfilling life.

1

Harry Burleigh (left) with his brother and grandfather.

As a young adult, he repeatedly attempted to escape from bondage—adventure stories Harry and Reginald heard time and again. He also attempted to educate himself. Slaveholders were determined to keep slaves from reading. On one occasion, a spelling book was discovered hidden under Hamilton's jacket; the punishment was seventy lashes with a knotted bullwhip. Later, after his eyesight deteriorated, Hamilton was allowed to buy his freedom for fifty dollars. He purchased his mother's freedom for an additional five. A certificate of freedom, dated April 13, 1835, allowed him to travel without fear of slave catchers. The faded letters—Harry and Reginald had examined them many times—described a young man "about thirty two years of age . . . five feet eight inches in height and of a bright mulatto complexion . . . partially blind . . . orderly and intelligent."

Hamilton sang as they walked from block to block, moving south of the water toward tree-lined streets with comfortable homes. The easy rhythm of their work meshed with Hamilton's smooth baritone in plantation songs like "Go Down, Moses," with its message of freedom:

> When Israel was in Egypt's land,
> Let my people go.
> Oppressed so hard they could not stand,
> Let my people go.
>
> Go down, Moses,
> Way down in Egypt's land.
> Tell old Pharaoh
> To let my people go!

Hamilton had purchased his freedom before the Civil War began in 1861. Notwithstanding his poor eyesight, he managed to succeed in a series of odd jobs. He pressed men's clothes, which required only an iron, a board, and a keen sense of touch. He was town crier, calling out news and announcements—work for which his strong, melodious voice was well suited. He raised a family and built a house in which three generations of Burleighs lived together. He also once helped to smuggle three runaway slaves to the house of Frank Henry, a white "conductor" for the Underground Railroad. The three fugitives crossed Lake Erie into Canada, and into freedom.

Waters's first daughter, Elizabeth, was Harry's mother. She attended college in Pittsburgh, graduating with an impressive command of French and a mission to assist others. In Erie she taught Sunday school at St. Paul's Episcopal Church, where her students were white. It was the largest Bible class in town. But she was denied employment in the public schools—except as a janitor in Public School No. 1.

Young Harry had a variety of jobs, including lamp-lighting, in his grandfather's footsteps. He and Reginald used their earnings to buy schoolbooks. Erie was a relatively tolerant place, whose black population—mostly unskilled laborers, waiters, cooks, and barbers—was too small to be regarded as a threat. Even so, at Erie Central High School Harry was frequently taunted for his black skin.

Home and church were Harry's chief supports. Both were filled with music. Elizabeth and Harry had inherited Hamilton's knack for song, and Harry, like Hamilton, was known to sing everywhere he went. On East Third Street, there were impromptu family concerts of slave songs, church hymns, and Stephen Foster songs. At St. Paul's, the hymn books included tunes by Haydn and Beethoven. Harry was also a member of the St. Paul's Boys' Choir. And he was in demand as a popular vocal soloist at the Park Presbyterian Church, the First Presbyterian Church, and the Hebrew Synagogue.

In these preradio days, such amateur music making supplied the main opportunity for music listening. Occasionally Erie was visited by famous musicians in the course of their national tours. Some would perform at the Erie Park Opera House. But, as elsewhere, there were also elegant private concerts in wealthy homes—such as that of Erie's Robert Russell. Elizabeth Burleigh would assist as a maid at Mrs. Russell's locally celebrated musicales.

Among the pianists to appear in the Russell home were the Hungarian Rafael Joseffy and the Venezuelan Teresa Carreño. Harry could not bear the thought of missing a chance to hear the celebrated Joseffy, who had studied in Germany with the most famous of all pianists: Franz Liszt. But he had no way of obtaining an invitation. He stood in snow up to his knees in order to watch and hear through a window as Joseffy raced through the Gypsy melodies of a Liszt Hungarian Rhapsody. The sapphire studs on the pianist's white cuffs glistened in the gaslight. The large, plush parlor, with its colored Tiffany windows, golden wallpaper, and alabaster statues, was itself more glamorous and romantic than any room Harry had ever seen. He lost track of the time and the cold. Days later, after he had fallen ill and almost caught pneumonia, he told his mother what he had done.

Elizabeth Burleigh asked Mrs. Russell if she could find a job for her son the next time she presented a concert. And so Harry was made a white-coated doorman for the Carreño recital. He greeted the guests, emptied ashtrays, and offered cigarettes. His mother, in white apron and cap, served liqueurs. The room swirled with expensive odors and animated chatter. Finally, Mrs. Russell clapped her hands, and Carreño strode, regal and smiling, to the grand piano. Joseffy had impressed with his finesse. But Harry was unprepared for the intensity of Carreño's chords and octaves, which she seemed to shake from her billowing sleeves. For others in the room, listening to Carreño was only entertainment. But Harry, standing in the back in his borrowed finery, devoured the music with a hunger he could not control.

On another occasion, Harry hid in the Opera House for an entire afternoon in order to hear a touring opera company headed by the Italian tenor

Italo Campanini. Harry had never heard an opera before. But he already lived for music. He resolved to become a professional musician—a singer.

In 1892, at the age of twenty-five, Harry Burleigh left Erie for New York City in his best mended clothes. He carried a suitcase in his hand and a precious train ticket in his pocket. Erie's leading citizens had contributed to a subscription fund to help him afford this lonely venture. In New York, according to plan, he auditioned for the National Conservatory of Music, which offered free tuition to African Americans of talent. The judges included Rafael Joseffy, who seemed more intimidating and less glamorous than in Mrs. Russell's salon. Harry was asked to sing passages at sight and to perform a song of his choice. Joseffy himself rose to deliver the verdict: an "A" for sight-reading, a "B" for voice; the candidate was "promising" but underprepared.

Harry thanked the judges and left the room, numb with disappointment. He was rescued from the shame of returning to Erie by a coincidence: on the way out, he recognized the conservatory's registrar, Frances Knapp MacDowell, as the kind-faced lady who had accompanied Teresa Carreño to Erie. (Her famous son, the American composer and pianist Edward MacDowell, had studied with Carreño in Germany.) Mrs. MacDowell remembered the white-coated doorman and successfully intervened on his behalf. This stroke of luck changed Harry Burleigh's life.

At the time Harry Burleigh entered the National Conservatory, most of the music we today call "American"—jazz, Broadway, soul, country-and-western—had not yet been born. Germany, France, and Italy had their own peasant and folk songs, symphonies and operas. If America's "sound," in comparison, remained largely undefined, there were two obvious reasons. The first was sociological: the United States was bigger, younger, and more diverse than any European nation, and it had recently been fractured by the Civil War. The second reason was logistical: before radio, the movies, and television, American music was a patchwork. New England had its distinctive church hymns. The farmers and miners of Kentucky's Appalachian Mountains sang ballads passed down by their forebears in England. The western plains produced lazy cowboy songs. The Creoles of New Orleans specialized in exuberant dances. But none of this music had acquired a national audience.

America already had its popular performers. The most famous touring bandmaster was Patrick Gilmore, whose own compositions included the Civil War favorite "When Johnny Comes Marching Home." After Gilmore's death in 1892, he was succeeded by John Philip Sousa, whose stirring marches included a veritable second national anthem: "The Stars and Stripes Forever." The best-known touring classical conductor, Theodore Thomas, traveled coast to coast introducing Americans to the masterpieces of Beethoven and Wagner. But as of 1900, no famous musician had attained the influence or instantaneous celebrity that broadcasts and recordings would soon make possible.

What would most bring unity to this American musical tapestry in the century to come was the same remarkable African American heritage that produced the slave songs Hamilton Burleigh sang to Harry. They had been passed from generation to generation before being written down and published in the 1860s. As "spirituals," they had become the most familiar of all American folk songs. And the most widely known of all American popular songs—those of Stephen Foster—bore their stamp. Foster was white, but such favorite Foster minstrel songs as "Old Folks at Home," "Oh! Susannah," and "Camptown Races," composed at midcentury, were initially sung by banjo-plucking white performers in blackface, their features and hands darkened by burned cork, their gestures and vocal inflections a caricature of African American sorrow or jubilation:

Way down upon de Swanee Ribber,
Far, far away,
Dere's wha my heart is turning ebber,
Dere's wha de old folks stay.

All up and down de whole creation,
Sadly I roam,

Still longing for de old plantation,
And for de old folks at home.

Blackface minstrelsy, a raucous variety show including topical speeches and spoofs, was wildly popular
in both North and South—but as the twentieth century approached, both blackface and minstrelsy were
on the wane. Foster, long dead, was still the most
popular American songwriter, but his "Jeannie with
the Light Brown Hair" and "My Old Kentucky
Home" now sounded quaint. The stage was set for
ragtime, gospel, and jazz—all part of a continuing
African American lineage. Along the way, spirituals
would be sung next to European art songs by great
vocalists in recital, and the most famous symphony
composed on American soil would embody slave
song. These landmark contributions would be made
by Harry Burleigh and by his friend and mentor
Antonín Dvořák.

Chapter 1

New York Greets Dvořák

The sun was setting on the Atlantic Ocean. A large German steamship passed the lighthouse at Sandy Hook en route to New York Harbor. On board, the passengers stood shoulder to shoulder along the side rails. Among them was a man of middle age, vigorous and erect. He wore a black homburg hat cocked at an angle. His necktie was emerald green. His vest was powder blue. His jacket and pants were finespun and freshly pressed. Wild reddish whiskers covered the man's face. His nose was broad, his complexion swarthy. His jet black eyes were clever and fiery. He looked like a peasant in fashionable city clothes.

The man was accompanied by another half his age, and by a woman, obviously his wife. Pressed against the latter, on either side, were two children— a boy and a girl. All were attired in their Sunday best.

Squeezing his dark eyes, the man peered intently at a distant object, a gigantic, green statue rising from the water. "The *Sta*tue of *Li*berty," he said.

"The Statue of Liberty," repeated the younger man—who, as it happened, was teaching him English.

"*Socha Svobody,*" the man translated, for the benefit of his wife and children. They nodded.

Now the man glanced to his right, to peruse another gigantic, distant object: the largest and strangest bridge he had ever seen, supported by cables strung from massive, brown pylons. Spanning a river clogged with masts and smokestacks, it was high enough for even the tallest ship to pass underneath.

"The Booklyn Bridge," said Antonín Dvořák.

"The *Brooklyn* Bridge," corrected Josef Kovařík.

"*Brooklynský Most.*"

Anna Dvořák and the children, fourteen-year-old Otilka and nine-year-old Antonín, gaped.

Dvořák now turned his attention to the most awesome sight of all, surmounting the congested harbor: an island skyline. Not spires and rooftops, as in Prague, but wall upon tall wall of stone. The walls glided nearer, disclosing thousands of illuminated windows. The boat forked left, away from the big bridge, up a river of such girth that no bridge could span it. Its eastern shore was packed with piers and with immense factories and warehouses. To the west, it was rimmed by a massive rockface.

Novy Svet. The New World.

Manhattan as Dvořák first saw it.

The SS *Saale* proceeded up the Hudson River and docked on the New Jersey side, in Hoboken. On a pier, a surging delegation of expectant Czechs was shouting: *"Vitejte!" "Sláva!"*

"Sláva!" shouted Kovařík. Anna Dvořák and the children beamed. Dvořák felt a lump in his throat; he merely waved.

The celebrating Czechs engulfed Dvořák's party of five. Out of the sea of bodies emerged a man screaming, "Dr. Dvořák! Dr. Dvořák!" This was Edmund Stanton from New York's National Conservatory of Music, who upon shaking hands attempted a greeting in Czech: *"Dobrý den!"* Stanton escorted his guests through customs, then, leaving the crowd of Czechs behind, to a ferry that crossed over to Manhattan. Dvořák watched the great island approach. As the ferry docked, he girded himself, a human particle about to be swept into a maelstrom of energy and sound.

From the carriage that now conveyed him toward his new lodgings, Dvořák surveyed the passing scene. He saw (for the first time) black people, and others obviously Chinese. This was the city with more Irish than Dublin and more Germans than Munich or Hamburg, with forty-three daily newspapers in six languages (including six in German and two in Czech), with half a million new immigrants each year.

The night was illuminated. Signs blazed with advertisements. The avenues were lined with shimmering window displays—and also with forests of utility poles groaning under as many as 200 wires. The horse-drawn carriages and cabs had ornamental lamps—yellow eyes—on either side. Multicolored electric trolleys passed at rapid intervals. Most amazing to Dvořák were the elevated trains, which arrived and departed as frequently as once a minute.

As a nine-year-old, he had been thrilled to see a railroad train pass through his Bohemian village like a visitor from another world. He became a dedicated train spotter. But never before had he seen locomotives on rails sixty feet off the ground, chugging through neighborhoods, spewing soot and cinders, belching plumes of flame and steam. He observed the dainty green stations of the Sixth Avenue "El," like cottages with iron roofs. And he endured with keen displeasure the shriek and clatter, and shrill grinding of the wheels, of these little trains.

The carriage reached Union Square, the hub of musical New York. Shouting amid the din, Stanton pointed out Chickering Hall and Steinway Hall—New York's two most important concert auditoriums excepting the new music hall Andrew Carnegie had built uptown on Fifty-seventh Street. They drove by the National Conservatory, then passed the Academy of Music—New York's leading opera house prior to the opening of the Metropolitan Opera ten years before.

Kovařík was translating intermittently for Anna and the children, fighting the clamor of hard hooves on cobblestone, of horse-car gongs, of the rattling wooden or metallic wheels of carriages and wagons. Dvořák was wondering how anyone could live or work in such a place.

They wound up at the Clarendon Hotel, on Eighteenth Street, in a large suite—everything in this city was large—with fresh flowers in every room.

Union Square in Dvořák's time.

Anna began inspecting the apartment. Stanton handed an envelope to Kovařík. Dvořák stepped to a large window and took in the view. Stuyvesant Park was teeming with people of all ages. He could dimly discern the accents of foreign tongues.

"Master, look at this!" Kovařík was waving some newspaper and magazine articles, courtesy of Stanton. "The Coming of Dvořák," read Kovařík. "From the *Daily Tribune.* Here's another one, from the *Times:* 'An interesting character is about to present himself

to music lovers in New York. It is due to the energy of Mrs. Thurber that New York's National Conservatory of Music is to have for its head next month Dr. Antonín Dvořák, the Bohemian composer, whose works are well known to English concertgoers and by no means unknown to those of our large cities.' Look, it shows how to pronounce your name."

Dvořák glanced at the clipping. Kovařík's finger was pointing at the word "Dvorzhak."

"And here's an entire magazine article: 'Antonín Dvořák' by Henry Edward Krehbiel. It calls your life 'a story of manifest destiny, of signal triumph over obstacle and discouraging environment. To rehearse it stimulates hope, reanimates ambition, and helps to keep alive popular belief in the reality of that precious attribute called genius.'"

Dvořák's English had improved considerably since Kovařík had begun tutoring him over the summer, but this was too much.

"What is he talking about?"

"He is suggesting that you are like an American— a 'self-made man.'"

"'Self-made man'?"

"That you grew up without special privileges. That you worked hard to achieve all you could with the gifts God gave you."

"This is true."

"And then he writes: 'In Dvořák and his work is to be found encouragement for the group of native musicians whose accomplishments of late have seemed to herald the rise of a school of American composers. Dvořák's example turns attention again to the wealth of material which lives in the vast mines of folk music.'"

"The *mines* of folk music?"

"He means that just as you draw inspiration from our folk music, so will American composers draw inspiration from their folk music."

"Who is this writer?"

"Tonik! This hotel costs fifty-five dollars a week!" This was Anna, in Czech, and steaming. "We cannot afford this kind of luxury. You must promise me, when you see Mrs. Thurber, you must explain, you must ask her to find . . ."

"Yes, yes. I see her October first, in just a few days. These rooms are too noisy anyway."

After church on the morning of October 1, Dvořák fetched Kovařík and headed for the National Conservatory, on East Seventeenth Street. Whenever he was in the city—any city—he disliked going out alone.

Dvořák knew Jeannette Thurber from their extensive negotiations, via letter and cable, regarding his payment and duties in New York—negotiations that resulted in an astronomical $15,000 salary, exceeding by one-third that of the mayor of New York. He knew that she had attended the Paris Conservatory of Music and returned to New York determined to create an American conservatory of comparable excellence and prestige so that gifted young Americans would not be tempted to study in Berlin, Vienna, and other Germanic musical capitals. Only that way, she reasoned, could Americans fashion symphonies and sonatas that sounded less "German" than what John Knowles Paine and Edward MacDowell were producing. She married Francis Beattie Thurber, a food merchant of great wealth and generosity. With his loyal support, and a list of backers including Andrew Carnegie and William K.

Vanderbilt, she established the National Conservatory in downtown Manhattan in 1885. The course of study was rigorous. The faculty was distinguished. Scholarships were provided for needy applicants. In fact, Mrs. Thurber sought out African American students. This priority was both philanthropic and practical: through plantation song, she believed, American concert music would acquire an American accent.

Dvořák had of course heard of Jeannette Thurber's charm and beauty. When she rose to greet him in her office, these reports were confirmed. Her luminous complexion dramatized her dark hair and eloquent, dark eyes. She was joined by Stanton, who looked like a businessman; by a second gentleman with a black goatee and an eager expression (a reporter, thought Dvořák); and a third man, very tall and theatrical, with spectacles, ironic eyes, and a comical paunch.

"Welcome to the National Conservatory, Dr. Dvořák," Mrs. Thurber began, folding his right hand in both of hers. "And thank you *so much* for the photographs and autographs you mailed."

"The pleasure is mine," Dvořák replied stiffly. (He hated courtesies.) "This is my assistant, Mr. Kovařík, who teaches me English the best he can. He is what you call a 'Czech American,' from Iowa. We met in Prague in summer, and I insisted he become my New York companion."

"I am delighted to meet you, Mr. Kovařík. May I present Mr. Stanton, whom I believe you already know. And this is Mr. James Creelman, my press secretary and a distinguished correspondent for the *Herald*. And this is Mr. James Gibbons Huneker, one of our leading music critics and a teacher of piano here at the conservatory."

Hands were shaken all around.

"Dr. Dvořák, we all want to know your first impressions of America," said Creelman in a rapid burst of words. "And your impressions of American music."

"This question is of course premature. In fact, Mrs. Thurber, the matter most upon my mind is the lodgings, the hotel, which is very expensive and, I am afraid, rather noisy. Would it be possible, with your assistance, to move to other quarters?"

"Please be assured that it is my privilege to assist you in all your needs. I will have Mr. Stanton take care of it. In fact, he will meet with you now to discuss your composition class and the concerts you will be conducting this semester. After that, I thought you might enjoy some afternoon refreshment with Mr. Huneker. He happens to be our leading local raconteur, as well as a connoisseur of the eating and drinking establishments in this vicinity."

Dvořák endured the meeting with Stanton. Then, dismissing Kovařík, he joined Huneker at Goerwirz's, a restaurant where German was spoken and the patrons—all of them men—consumed more drink than food. Huneker inquired if Dvořák had ever tasted a whiskey cocktail. He had not. He tried one, then another. Huneker observed that Dvořák was in a drinking mood.

"Shall we explore the great thirst belt, Doctor? This neighborhood is an imbiber's *paradiso.*"

Dvořák next found himself at a place called Maurer's. After that came Moulds'. Huneker marveled at his new friend's capacity for cocktails. He decided to attempt a conversation about music.

"They tell me, Dr. Dvořák, that you are a great friend of Brahms. What manner of man is he?"

"An atheist," replied Dvořák, sipping his sixth cocktail of the day. His face had reddened perceptibly. His eyes retained their ferocity. He looks like a pirate, Huneker decided.

"Do you know Dr. Seidl? He is our great maestro here. Also an atheist of long standing. He delights in trampling proper Christian sensitivities. His only god is Wagner, with whom he actually resided as a young man."

"Another anti-Christian," said Dvořák. "But a great composer."

Six beers had wonderfully lubricated Huneker's silver tongue. "Yes, Doctor, Wagner's opera *Parsifal* preaches a dozen half-baked religions, does it not? Give me *Tristan und Isolde*—now that is a magnificent Wagnerian brew. How it searches and sears the nerves! To hear Dr. Seidl conduct it is one of life's profoundest pleasures. How he does summon the elemental groundswell from the vasty deep! And the doctor himself—Seidl, I mean—is a baton incarnate. *Der grosse Schweiger*—the great silent one—is what we call him. He is the proverbial sphinx, possessor of the eye omniscient. Why, when he is silent, you can almost hear him thinking."

Dvořák listened.

"What do you say, Doctor, to a trip to Fleischmann's? That is Seidl's very lair. You can meet the great man himself."

Seidl was not to be found at Fleischmann's Viennese Bakery, Café, and Restaurant at Broadway and Tenth Street. But Huneker did encounter Victor Herbert, who was Seidl's principal cellist at both the New York Philharmonic and the Metropolitan Opera, as well as a leading local composer and a faculty member at the National Conservatory. Herbert proved a chubby, round-faced man. He was thrilled to meet Dvořák. Did Dvořák think America could foster a "national school" of composers, comparable to the Bohemian school? Herbert wanted to know.

Dvořák pondered the question. He then took a sip of whiskey and said, "It is to the poor that I turn for greatness in music. The poor people, they work hard and seriously. I was myself the son of peasants. I grew with my feet planted in the soil. The folk music is deep inside me. That is what American composers must also feel."

"But Dr. Dvořák, America is not a land of peasants," Herbert responded. "There are, however, the Negro

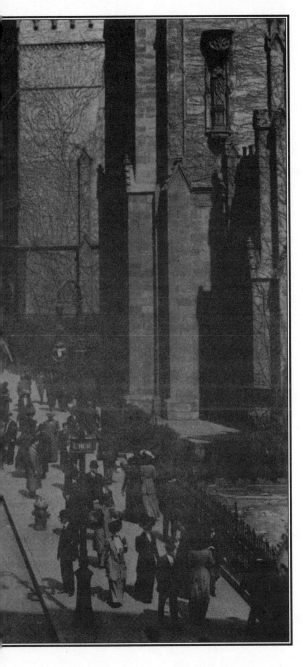

Broadway at East Tenth Street, where Dvořák and Seidl met daily.

melodies—the plantation songs of the South. Mrs. Thurber puts great stock in those. She expects you to write an American symphony, by the way. She expects you to point us in the proper direction."

"This puts the cart before the horse," Dvořák said. "In Bohemia, every schoolmaster teaches singing and violin, also organ for Mass. We examine children at an early age and choose the right instrument. Every man plays. There are very many professional musicians. I myself three times received the Austrian State Stipend. This was the government's way of supporting talented, young artists who could not yet support themselves. We do not have to beg the rich to support the music schools, as Mrs. Thurber must do."

"My good Doctor, that is the American way." Huneker's speech had slowed and thickened. "And as for Negro melodies being native to the soil, there were, I trust, no black men in these parts when Signor Columbus set anchor."

"You have your Indians," said Dvořák. "I myself have read *The Song of Hiawatha* by Henry Wadsworth Longfellow. This poem is actually well known in Europe."

"But the Indians have no folk music, Doctor. Just chants and tom-toms. Primitive stuff. You will be better off with the Negro melodies after all."

"How can I hear these Negro melodies?"

"I will procure a book for your pleasure. Meanwhile, it would be prudent to ingest some food, *nicht wahr?* Suppose you, Mr. Herbert, and I requisition *Bratwurst und Kartofeln* for the table?"

"Eat? Let us instead drink slivovitz. I already know the place for it, on Houston Street. It will warm you after so much beer."

Huneker was in no condition to travel. Dvořák and Herbert took their leave.

"Such a man is as dangerous to a moderate drinker as a false beacon is to a shipwrecked sailor," quipped James Gibbons Huneker, to no one in particular.

Dear Sir, Esteemed Madam,

I have been wanting to write to you for a long time but have always put it off, waiting for a more suitable moment when I could tell my Prague friends something of particular interest about America and especially about the musical conditions here. It is all so new and interesting that I cannot put everything down on paper, and so I will limit myself to the most important things.

The first and chief thing is that, thanks be to God, we are all well and liking it here. The journey was lovely except for one day when everybody but me was sick. The view from Sandy Hook of New York and the Statue of Liberty (in whose head alone there is room for sixty persons and where banquets are often held) is most impressive! And then the amount of shipping from all parts of the world! As I say, amazing.

The city itself is magnificent, lovely buildings and beautiful streets. It is expensive. At first we paid fifty-five dollars a week for three rooms. We are now in a flat on East Seventeenth Street, just four minutes from the National Conservatory, and very satisfied. Mr. Steinway sent a piano immediately, free of charge, so we have at least one nice piece of furniture in our sitting room. Besides this we have three other rooms and a small room and pay eighty dollars a month. A lot for us, but the normal price here.

On Sunday, Oct. 9, there was a Czech concert in my honor. Three thousand people were present in the hall, with no end to the cheering and clapping. There were speeches in Czech and English, and I, poor creature, had to make a speech of thanks from the platform, holding a silver wreath in my hands.

Only three days later the festivities began in celebration of Columbus's arrival in the New World. We have never seen anything like it; I think that even the Americans have not seen anything like it. Imagine row after row of processions representing industry, artisans, engineers, artists, and all else. And it lasted more than three days from morning until 2 A.M., without interruption. Thousands and thousands of people, and so many different kinds of music! Every minute something new happened. People stood on the rooftops of buildings eleven stories high.

What the American papers write about me is simply terrible. They see in me, they say, the savior of American music and I don't know what else besides! I am to show them to the promised land of a new and independent art—in short, to create a national music. If the small Czech nation can have such composers, they say, why could not they, too, when their country and people are so immense?

Dvořák and family members in New York, with Anna Dvořák seated.

Forgive me for lacking a little in modesty, but I am only telling you what the American papers are constantly writing. It is certainly both a great and a splendid task for me, and I hope that with God's help I shall accomplish it. There is more than enough material. We have pupils from as far away as San Francisco. They are mostly poor, but at our school anybody who is really talented pays no fee! I myself have only eight pupils, some of whom are very promising.

The composers are all much the same as at home, brought up in the German school, but here and there another spirit, another coloring, flashes forth—something Indian. I am very curious how things will develop. These Americans are practical and hardworking: they will fashion something of their own. As regards my own work, there is not a great deal of it. Mrs. Thurber is very considerate, as she wrote to me in Europe that she would be.

I must stop. My kind regards to yourself and your wife.

I remain,

Gratefully yours,

Antonín Dvořák

My wife, who is with me, asks to be remembered to you as well.

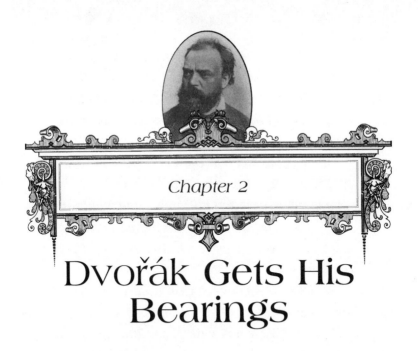

Dvořák Gets His Bearings

Dearest Papa,

Life with Master Dvořák in New York has now settled into a routine. He teaches for two hours every Tuesday, Thursday, and Saturday. This is fewer hours than he originally planned, and he is pleased to have more time for his own work. Every morning: church, for he thanks God for his every blessing. At night, cards: Darda, just like at home. I still sometimes administer my English lessons, though they are hardly necessary any longer. But I am his constant companion. He dislikes even to cross the street alone. The crowds and the noise disturb him. Remember, more than one million people live in New York City!

Mrs. Dvořák and the children are doing well. But, as you know, there are another four children left behind in Prague, and the Master often longs for them. He also misses his pigeons and locomotives. But he has found modest American substitutes.

One day we went to the Central Park, which stretches from 59th to 110th Street and includes all manner of trees and hills, lakes and fountains. The statues include one of Beethoven and Cleopatra's Needle, an Egyptian monument over thirty centuries old.

We found a small Zoological Garden and buildings with different kinds of birds. And then we came to a huge aviary with about 200 pigeons. It was a great surprise for the Master, and his pleasure at seeing the pigeons was great—even though none could compare with his Bohemian "pouters" and "fantails" at home. We now make the trip to Central Park at least once and often twice a week. Meanwhile, in his New York apartment there are birdcages everywhere, with the doors left open. The thrushes fly from room to room while the Master composes.

With locomotives it is a more difficult matter. In New York there is only one station, the Grand Central Depot. The others are across the river. Grand Central is indescribably large. The train-shed, which has a curved glass-and-tin roof, holds twelve parallel tracks. But nobody is allowed onto the platforms except the passengers.

The aviary in the Central Park Zoo.

We beg the porters in vain to let us look at the "American locomotive." So we must travel by overhead tram to 155th Street, a good hour from the Master's house. There, on a bank, we wait for the Chicago or Boston express to go by. It takes up a lot of time, nearly an entire afternoon, as we always wait for a number of trains so that it is worth the journey.

And now the Master has found a new hobby: steamships. For one thing, the harbor is much nearer than 155th Street. And on the day of departure the public is allowed on board, an opportunity the Master makes full use of. Every morning, the Master's first work is to take the Herald *and read the shipping news. It is said that 3,000 steamships arrive in New York harbor from foreign ports every year. But it seems that there is not a boat that we have not inspected from stem to stern. The Master always starts a conversation with the ship's captain or with his assistants. And so in a short time we have come to know all the captains and mates by name. And when a ship is due to sail, we go there and watch it from the shore till it is out of sight.*

Sometimes the Master remains a little longer than usual at the conservatory, or is so engrossed in his work at home that there is no longer time to go to the harbor. Then we travel by overhead tram to Battery Park, at the southern tip of Manhattan, and from there follow the ship for as long as it remains in sight. We also track the incoming ships. When one is late there is confusion and weeping at the dock. The Master grows worried himself, and we must watch until the ship appears on the horizon. The Master grows especially homesick on steamer days. His thoughts of home often move him to tears. I am certain that he is thinking not only of his dear ones left behind, but also of his three firstborn children, all of whom perished at very early ages.

In general, the Master prefers not to visit unfamiliar places. He enjoys the company of Dr. Anton Seidl, the famous conductor, and likes to attend Dr. Seidl's New York Philharmonic concerts. But only once have we visited the great Metropolitan Opera House—for Wagner's Siegfried, *which the Master had never heard. It seats more than 3,500 people. We found ourselves among the "Diamond Horseshoe" boxes for the very fashionable. Of course, we wore our best and darkest suits. But everywhere were ill-behaved gentlemen in tuxedos and ladies showing off their gowns and diamonds. We felt like hiding in the back. We left after the first act.*

Though the Master is kindness itself, he has a ferocious appearance with his wild hair and eyes. With his students he is like a father, strict but affectionate. Everyone talks about the time he used his foot to grind a student's composition on the floor, grunting like a wild boar—and how he next tenderly picked up the papers and said something kind as an afterthought.

I have not shared this with him yet, but I have decided to invite the Master and his entire family to spend the summer with us in Spillville. He will feel perfectly at home among our Czech American

*neighbors and friends. The Iowa air will refresh him.
And you will find him a memorable companion.
He never puts on the airs of a "great man."*

Kisses to Mama and the children,

Your devoted son,

Josef

Josef Kovařík.

The Columbus Day celebrations Dvořák had witnessed shortly after arriving in New York—the three days of parades and flag-waving festivities—gave him plenty to think about. Americans were intensely patriotic; but what was an "American"?

Dvořák was also patriotic. He was born in 1841 in a village eighteen miles north of the Bohemian capital, Prague. Today, Prague lies in the Czech Republic. In Dvořák's time, it was part of the Hapsburg Empire, based in Vienna. In 1867, the empire became a dual monarchy with two seats of power: German-speaking Vienna and Hungarian Budapest. Both Germans and Hungarians looked down on the empire's minority Slavs, including the Czechs—themselves a combination of Bohemians (like Dvořák) and Moravians. In fact, the word "Slav" was said to derive from the German *Sklave,* meaning

The house in which Dvořák was born.

Prague in 1885.

"slave." Unless they adopted German customs and speech, Slavs were considered barbarians.

Dvořák learned the violin at the age of five. "Tonik" played at his father's inn, at local churches, and in the village band. His father, a butcher, played the zither and composed simple dances. Fiddlers and pipers, polkas on the village green, singing at church and the tavern were part of daily life.

At the age of eleven Dvořák was taken out of school to become a butcher in the footsteps of his father and grandfather. But it was against his will. Five years later, his parents permitted him to depart on a hay cart for Prague, there to enroll in a genuine school of music. Dvořák now heard operas and symphonies for the first time. Too poor to buy tickets, he would sneak into concerts by concealing himself at the back of the stage, behind the drums. After graduating, he joined a band that played in restaurants. He composed on the side. He was too poor to rent a piano. He burned or discarded most of what he wrote.

Dvořák's struggle to become a composer was a struggle to find a creative voice of his own—a Bohemian voice, colored by the peasant polkas and waltzes he played and danced as a boy. But Dvořák's Bohemia was (like New York, with its German-trained composers and performers) a German musical colony. Even his Bohemian instructors in Prague had been required to teach in German, the language of Vienna. And

Young Dvořák.

Bohemian composers wrote symphonies indistinguishable from those of their German teachers and models.

In 1859—the same year Dvořák graduated from music school at the age of eighteen—the Hapsburgs were defeated in Italy. Emperor Francis Joseph's grip on the Hapsburg minorities began to weaken. Twelve years later, the emperor agreed to a triple monarchy that would place Bohemians on the same high footing as Hungarians. Objections in Budapest, and among Germans living in Bohemia, scuttled this scheme, inflaming Bohemian discontent. At the same time, the suppression of Czech language and culture diminished. In Prague, plans were laid for a national theater, where operas and plays would be given in Czech only. Three years later, the theater opened, and the band in which Dvořák played became the core of its new orchestra. For nine years Dvořák was exposed to German, Italian, and French opera and drama in Czech translation as well as to the first important operas composed in Czech, by his countryman Bedřich Smetana. Dvořák acquired a sense of mission: to help Smetana create Bohemian symphonies and operas.

All over Europe, in fact, nationalism was a growing force among musicians, writers, and painters. No less than political leaders, they were eager to throw off the influence of the great imperial powers. In Russia, where France was the language of the aristocracy, nationalist composers like Tchaikovsky and Rimsky-Korsakov fashioned a Russian style based on earthy peasant music. Liszt spiced his Hungarian Rhapsodies with devilish Gypsy fiddling.

In Prague, Dvořák joined the ranks of Europe's leading nationalists. His *Slavonic Dances,* published in 1878, were a sensation. The lilting tunes he used weren't actually sung by Slavic peasants, but they sounded as natural and spontaneous as folk music. Heard once, they were unforgettable. They brilliantly evoked swirling skirts and flirtatious smiles, wheezing bagpipes and rustic violins.

Initially published as piano duets—for two pianists sitting side by side—the *Slavonic Dances* were soon made available for all kinds of instruments, and to all kinds of people. Music shops ran out of copies. They were heard indoors and outdoors, in taverns and parlors, restaurants and concert halls. As orchestral works, they were performed in Boston as early as 1879. With radios and recordings yet to come, they became the hit tunes of their day.

In Prague, Dvořák had become so famous that his portrait could be seen on every major street. He was greeted by street vendors and shopkeepers. But his Viennese publisher, Fritz Simrock, wanted Dvořák to move from Prague to Vienna. And the leading Viennese music critic, Eduard Hanslick, wrote to Dvořák in 1882: "After such initial successes, your art requires a wider horizon, a German environment, a bigger, non-Czech public." This advice was well intentioned, but Dvořák was only too aware of the air of superiority of the Viennese. And Vienna itself, with its ring of monumental public buildings—the Parliament, the Opera, the University, the City Hall—all too obviously proclaimed its imperial supremacy. He stayed in Prague.

Dvořák also argued with Simrock over the publisher's practice of printing the titles of his works, as well as his first name, in German. Dvořák wanted the titles in both Czech and German, and his name given as "Ant."—an abbreviation equally appropriate for the Czech "Antonín" or the German "Anton." He wrote to Simrock in 1885: "An artist, too, has a fatherland in which he must have a firm faith and which he must love." He left Simrock five years later.

And so it was that Dvořák came to America having conquered the musical capitals of Europe. His music appealed to Americans like Jeannette Thurber not only because it was tuneful and grand, but because of its local roots. Dvořák represented a potential model for American composers seeking, as Dvořák himself had sought, to escape foreign influences.

Dvořák instantly identified with the American cause: he understood the dilemma of the cultural underdog. He saw and heard that American composers trained in Germany were stuck in German ways, just as Bohemian composers had been. But the Americans had a special problem. Bohemian musicians, writers, and artists could base their art on the Czech language, on traditional Czech folk tales and costumes, lullabies and ballads. What were America's traditions?

Americans were themselves colonizers. The native inhabitants of North America had languages and customs of their own. The predominant language of the American colonies was English, acquired from abroad. The men and women who settled Plymouth, New Amsterdam, Pennsylvania, and Virginia were also Dutch or African. Wave upon wave of immigration followed: Americans were Protestants, Catholics, and Jews. They were German, Irish, and Italian. They were white, red, or black. The Hapsburg Empire was a collection of nationalities in the process of breaking up; the United States was a collection of nationalities trying to fit together. In New York, Dvořák quickly found himself subject to a daily barrage of advice and encouragement. Jeannette Thurber and James Creelman were urging him to write an "American" symphony. James Huneker had (as promised) provided an article on "Negro melodies." Henry Krehbiel, of the *Tribune,* would mail Dvořák particularly promising specimens of both African American and Native American music, with his best wishes.

Dvořák felt challenged and intrigued. At the same time, he needed a refuge from his American acquaintances. He found one at Fleischmann's Restaurant, which he had first visited with Huneker in search of Anton Seidl. And Seidl became Dvořák's closest New York friend, to whom he could confide his fundamental questions about America's musical prospects.

One topic that united Seidl and Dvořák was democracy. Dvořák loathed the Viennese aristocrats who lorded over the Hapsburg dominions. Seidl refused to return to the German opera houses that bid for his services. America was the promised land where millionaires worked as hard as farmers, where porters and guests in even the best hotels addressed one another as "Mister." It was Seidl's conviction that "the man who resists playing classical works for common people is not a true American." Like Jeannette Thurber, he lamented the absence of government grants for orchestras and conservatories, as in Europe. But private wealth was plentiful, as were private individuals dedicated to the arts. In New York, Andrew Carnegie had built his new music hall. In Boston, Henry Higginson paid for the Boston Symphony—a great orchestra, comparable to the best anywhere.

To Dvořák's way of thinking, America's fine cultural attire—its New York Philharmonic, Boston Symphony, and Metropolitan Opera—was essentially borrowed from Berlin and Vienna, Paris and Milan. There would be no American composers to set beside Beethoven and Mozart—or even beside Tchaikovsky and Dvořák—until an American school was formulated. Thurber, Huneker, and Krehbiel all put stock in Negro melodies. In his National Conservatory class, Dvořák placed high hopes in an African American student, Maurice Arnold, who had composed a set of *American Plantation Dances* for orchestra. But he would exert his most productive influence on another black musician, in whom the Negro melodies lived and breathed.

One day Dvořák received a note informing him of a first-year student at the National Conservatory, an African American from Pennsylvania. He was not a candidate for Dvořák's composition class—his technical knowledge of music was still weak. But it had been arranged that Dvořák would hear him sing.

Young Harry Burleigh.

The day arrived and with it, in Dvořák's office, a
young man with a mustache. He met Dvořák's gaze
with frankness and respect.

"Are you Mr. Harry Burleigh?"

"Yes, Doctor, I am he."

"And what do you plan to sing for me this morning?"

"I plan to sing 'Go Down, Moses,'" said Harry Burleigh, who sat down at Dvořák's piano and proceeded to sing it. His voice was a firm and resonant baritone. He enunciated every word distinctly, with meaning and force:

When Israel was in Egypt's land,
Let my people go.
Oppressed so hard they could not stand,
Let my people go.

Go down, Moses,
Way down in Egypt's land.
Tell old Pharaoh
To let my people go!

Thus saith the Lord, bold Moses said,
Let my people go,
If not I'll smite your firstborn dead,
Let my people go!

Go down, Moses,
Way down in Egypt's land.
Tell old Pharaoh
To let my people go!

"That is most impressive, Mr. Burleigh. Most inspirational. The melody is worthy of Beethoven, I would say. Do you care to sing another?"

Burleigh now sang his favorite song—slowly, solemnly, softly, like a hymn.

> Deep river,
> My home is over Jordan.
> Deep river, Lord,
> I want to cross over into campground.
>
> Oh, don't you want to go
> To that gospel feast,
> That promised land where all is peace?
>
> Oh deep river, Lord,
> I want to cross over into campground.

Dvořák's eyes were red. "Mr. Burleigh, the 'campground' in this song—is it death?"

"You could say that, Doctor. Or you might say that the Promised Land, across the Jordan River, is *freedom*. This song was sung by slaves in the South, before the Civil War. They couldn't sing openly about their heart's desire—to cross over to the North."

"How do you know this, Mr. Burleigh?"

"From my grandfather. He was born a slave. He tried to escape to freedom, but was captured every time. Then he purchased his freedom—for fifty dollars. He taught me many songs."

"Are you religious, Mr. Burleigh?"

"My family is devoted to church and to the Bible. We are all children of God."

"And we are all equal before the Lord, are we not, Mr. Burleigh?"

"Indeed."

"How were you able to afford to come to New York, to study music here at the conservatory?"

"Well, friends and neighbors helped out with the train fare. And Mrs. Thurber gave me a scholarship."

"Could you use some pocket money?"

"Oh, yes. I do odd jobs, but . . ."

"Can you copy music?"

"I have no special skill in that department. I could learn."

"Mr. Burleigh, would you like to be my assistant? I need a copyist, a musical secretary. But I would insist on one condition."

"What is that, Doctor?"

"You would have to sing for me—upon request."

"With pleasure, Doctor."

"Then I will be in touch with you."

Harry Burleigh could not resist a smile. Dvořák dismissed him abruptly. He sat at the piano and played "Deep River," harmonizing the tune as he might at church. Then he improvised a melody of his own, in the same style—an American plantation song without words, by Antonín Dvořák. He repeated it, elaborating the accompaniment as an orchestra might. The tune was like clay under his skilled fingers. And the clay was wonderfully firm and rich. Its possibilities were limitless, even . . . symphonic. "It is to the poor that I turn for musical greatness," Dvořák had told Victor Herbert.

Dvořák stopped and rested his head in his hands. The Lord was looking after his servant Dvořák—even in New York.

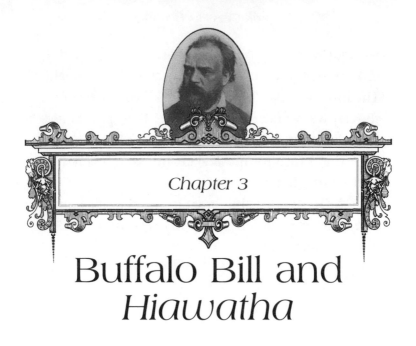

Chapter 3

Buffalo Bill and *Hiawatha*

"LADIES AND GENTLEMEN! Presenting Buffalo Bill's Wild West and Legions of Rough Riders of the World! An AUTHENTIC PAGEANT, with BUFFALO BILL, the Honorable WILLIAM F. CODY, repeating heroic parts played in actual life upon the American plains in days just past—upon the Western wilderness, and in DREAD and DANGEROUS scenes of SAVAGE and CRUEL warfare."

An elderly man costumed in leather, with shoulder-length white hair and a white mustache and goatee, circled the dirt arena on a white horse, waving a broad-brimmed white hat. Behind him, in parade, rode cavalrymen in smart blue uniforms, cowboys twirling lassos, and painted Indians with feathered war bonnets. The setting was Madison Square Garden, in the middle of New York City.

Buffalo Bill.

Dvořák had heard of Buffalo Bill. The touring "Wild West" was a major attraction in England and Europe. But the reality exceeded his expectations. Cody was a master showman. His entourage filled the vast indoor space with the clamor and smoke of horses, war cries, and gunshots. An offstage wind machine, driven by a steam engine using four six-foot fans, sent wagonloads of dry leaves swirling through the "settlers' camp"; it was also used to create a cyclone and a prairie fire. A detachment of real-life squaws assembled an "Indian camp," erecting tepees while their men smoked long-stem pipes and kept watch over a pair of paleface female "captives." Annie Oakley and Johnnie Baker shot glass balls out

The Wild West show.

of the air while on their backs or supported upside down.

Dvořák's fascination with Native Americans was typical of Europeans of his generation. Europe's first settlers had vanished countless centuries ago, but in America one could still encounter "primitive" native inhabitants who lived off the land. By 1892, when Dvořák attended the "Wild West" in the company of Jeannette Thurber, the Indian Wars had ended.

Six decades had passed since the Indian Removal Act forced over 90 percent of all Native Americans living east of the Mississippi River to relocate west. Custer's Last Stand—the last battle in which Native Americans emerged victorious—was a sixteen-year-old memory. Custer's enemies, the Sioux, had scattered into Canada. Other tribes were removed to reservations on lands not readily farmable. The buffalo they had hunted in great herds were nearly extinct. Two years before, the same Seventh Cavalry that Custer once led had massacred 300 defenseless Sioux at Wounded Knee, South Dakota.

The proud American Indian celebrated by Cody, roaming vast expanses of mountain and prairie, was already history, and yet tantalizingly recent. Dvořák, from Nelahozeves in Bohemia, now watched the Deadwood Stage Coach careen around the arena with a dozen warriors in pursuit. He watched Buck Taylor, "King of the Cowboys," subdue bucking horses and perform roping tricks. And he saw a reenactment of Custer's Last Stand, a climactic melee featuring actual participants from both sides, reunited as actors. Following the death of Custer (as played by Buck Taylor), Cody appeared amid the carnage as Custer's would-be rescuer. The lights dimmed, and an illuminated screen projected the words "TOO LATE."

More typically, of course, the Native Americans were shown driven away from the settlers' camp, the stagecoach, and other points of attack. With his years of close contact as a scout and Pony Express rider, Cody was not unsympathetic to their plight. In his show, he depicted the Sioux as a people of culture, patriotically defending their homeland. Once, in 1885, the Sioux spiritual leader Sitting Bull had actually been the star attraction. Rather than have him whoop and holler, Cody presented the old medicine man as a dignified survivor. He was announced, then rode alone into the arena as the crowd fell silent.

At the show Dvořák and Mrs. Thurber saw in 1892, banners proclaimed the Indian FORMER FOE— PRESENT FRIEND. The theme of reconciliation was supported by publicity stories of Seventh Cavalry veterans and Sioux warriors harmoniously keeping company as members of the "Wild West." But the new friendship was quite obviously not conducted on equal terms. The Indians had lost.

To Americans of Dvořák's time, the Native American was a nuisance or a fascination. The "red man" was abused, admired, ignored—and studied. Henry R. Schoolcraft pioneered in collecting tales and legends— "the bones of aboriginal lore"—beginning in the 1820s. A decade later, George Catlin pioneered in portraying Native Americans on canvas. Intoxicated by the fantastic attire and exotic customs of the tribesmen he encountered, he traveled by canoe where no other white man went. Eventually, he assembled his hundreds of paintings alongside a singular collection of paraphernalia—lances, robes, headdresses, even a twenty-five-foot-high tepee of painted buffalo skin. He successfully toured this "Indian Gallery," which also included live Native Americans and two grizzly bears. By the time it got to London and Paris, Catlin's show featured reenactments of rituals and encampments. Other artists followed suit with

George Catlin's portrait of Chief Clermont (1834).

touring galleries of their own. Buffalo Bill and his "Wild West" show were an outgrowth of these presentations.

At the same time, widespread recognition that the Native American was actually threatened with extinction spurred an upsurge of scholarly interest in tribal history and customs. Native American music—which no Native American had written down—was documented for the first time by a New Yorker named Theodore Baker in 1882.

But the most prominent advocate of Native American song was Dvořák's chief journalistic champion: Henry Krehbiel of the *New York Tribune*. Krehbiel's campaign for an American musical style was supported by vast scholarly knowledge. He was the first American to survey the folk music of Russians, Jews, Scandinavians, and "Orientals." His 155-page book *Afro-American Folksongs* was unprecedented in detail and scope. "American Indians," he observed, "have songs for all the solemn and festive functions of life: love songs and war songs; gambling songs; mystic chants with which the conjuring medicine man drives away disease and stills pain; songs of thanksgiving and songs of mourning." Essentially, this music was religious: "When an Indian sings, it is not for the sake of the beauty of the song."

Krehbiel's investigations took him to the Six Nations Reservation in Ontario, where he studied the ceremonial music of the Iroquois, an Indian nation in which he found "nobility of character and real moral and intellectual gentleness." In the music of the Kwakiutl Indians of Vancouver Island (which he encountered at the Chicago Columbian Exposition of 1893), he discovered complex rhythmic relationships between singing and drumming. Around the same time, he was able to avail himself of a new invention: he recorded the singing of Chief John Buck. When Buck died, Krehbiel wrote: "All that was mortal of him has passed away, but his voice lives, like another embodiment of his soul, to be conjured up at will, but freighted now with a deeper, gentler, sweeter emotion than it seemed to have when he was in the body. My phonographic cylinders are thus become monuments of two civilizations—that of the ancient red man, so imperfectly understood as yet even by those who have learned that the Indians were not the bloodthirsty savages depicted in trashy tales and shortsighted histories, and that of today marked by its wonders of mechanical ingenuity."

From one viewpoint, Native Americans were barbarians who practiced war dances and scalped settlers— primitives who stood in the way of progress. A popular western maxim said, "The only good Indian is a dead Indian." Many cultivated easterners, however, perceived instead "noble savages" uncorrupted by money, competition, anxiety, and other diseases of civilization—and yet doomed to extinction. When Krehbiel called them "savages," he meant not that they were bloody, but that they were premodern. Catlin thought many Native Americans led lives "much more happy than ours." He extolled their "silent and stoic dignity." And yet the Mandan settlement he admiringly painted was wiped out by the white man's smallpox five years later. Catlin deplored the "invasion" of the Native Americans' lands and the violation of their customs. He resolved "to rescue from oblivion" their dying culture "by the aid of my brush and my pen."

As Catlin romanticized the noble savage, other artists romanticized the virgin western terrain. Images of snowy mountain peaks, of towering waterfalls, of limitless buffalo herds and pastel sunsets, evoked nature sublime and monumental. The canvases of some artists were so panoramic—up to six feet high and twelve across—that connoisseurs used opera glasses to magnify tiny details that might turn out to be horses or tepees.

In literature, the most popular expression of the noble savage inhabiting a virgin wilderness was Henry Wadsworth Longfellow's *The Song of Hiawatha,* published in 1855. In a prologue, Longfellow addressed his 160-page epic poem to:

> Ye whose hearts are fresh and simple,
> Who have faith in God and nature,
> Who believe, that in all ages
> Every human heart is human,
> That in even savage bosoms
> There are longings, yearnings, strivings,
> For the good they comprehend not.

More than human, the Native Americans of *Hiawatha* are humane; to Longfellow, the Indian embodied "magnanimity, generosity, benevolence, and pure religion without hypocrisy." He lived in holy communion with nature.

By today's standards of historical accuracy, *The Song of Hiawatha* is of course not a truthful portrait. Even the name "Hiawatha"—a mythical Iroquois chief—is a confusion; the Schoolcraft tales Longfellow relied upon are Algonquin. But Longfellow did not attempt a correct rendering of Native American history or legend. Rather, his goal was to create an American epic: a legend, for all America, of New World origins. His success was such that 5,000 copies were sold in the first five weeks after publication, 45,000 by 1859. *Hiawatha* was chanted in costume. Steamboats and schools were named "Hiawatha." A New York saloon concocted a Hiawatha drink guaranteed "to make the imbiber fancy himself in the happy hunting ground."

And who is Hiawatha? Prophet and magician, child of the West Wind, he is dispatched by the Great Spirit to guide the Indian nations. His enchanted moccasins propel him through forest and prairie at supernatural speed. He talks with bears and beavers and fish. He soothes pain and conflict, inspires the nations to bury their weapons and smoke the pipe of peace. In a climactic duel, he defeats his rival, Pau-Puk-Keewis. The arrival of Christian missionaries, at the poem's close, coincides with Hiawatha's leave-taking:

In the glory of the sunset,
In the purple mists of evening,
To the regions of the home-wind,
Of the North-west wind, Keewaydin,
To the Islands of the Blessed,
To the kingdom of Ponemah,
To the land of the Hereafter!

Thus does Longfellow narrate a golden age of precivilization and its twilit end: the passing of a noble race.

The *Hiawatha* craze inspired *Hiawatha* music. By 1900, American and British composers had produced a *Hiawatha* overture, a *Hiawatha* suite, a *Hiawatha* symphony, a *Farewell of Hiawatha*, and *Hiawatha's Wedding Feast*. But by far the most enduring musical treatment was by the Bohemian Antonín Dvořák.

Dvořák had read *Hiawatha* in Czech translation decades before coming to New York. For him, it seemed a quintessential American fable. Its wholesomeness and solemnity appealed to his religious nature. And, no less than that of plantation song, the religiosity of Native American music stirred and impressed him.

It was Dvořák's dream to compose a *Hiawatha* opera. Three sections of *The Song of Hiawatha* especially appealed to his composer's imagination. They comprise a tragic love story.

In "Hiawatha's Wooing," Hiawatha visits the land of the Dacotahs and there meets Minnehaha, known as Laughing Water, loveliest of Dacotah women. He wins her hand and they depart:

Pleasant was the journey homeward,
Through interminable forests,
Over meadow, over mountain,
Over river, hill, and hollow.
Short it seemed to Hiawatha,
Though they journeyed very slowly,
Though his pace was checked and slackened
To the steps of Laughing Water.

At "Hiawatha's Wedding Feast," a grand ceremony pulsating with music, the Beggar's Dance is a central event. Pau-Puk-Keewis—idler, gambler, handsome "merry mischief-maker" versed "in all games of skill and hazard"—rises among the assembled guests:

He was dressed in shirt and doe-skin,
White and soft, and fringed with ermine,
All inwrought with beads of wampum;
He was dressed in deer-skin leggings,
Fringed with hedgehog quills and ermine,

And in moccasins of buck-skin
Thick with quills and beads embroidered.
On his head were plumes of swan's-down,
On his heels were tails of foxes,
In one hand a fan of feathers,
And a pipe was in the other.
Barred with streaks of red and yellow,
Streaks of blue and bright vermilion,
Shone the face of Pau-Puk-Keewis.
From his forehead fell his tresses,
Smooth and parted like a woman's,
Shining bright with oil, and painted,
Hung with braids of scented grasses . . .

The trancelike dance of Pau-Puk-Keewis—"to the sound of flutes and singing, to the sound of drums and voices"—begins slowly, "treading softly like a panther." Gradually, hypnotically, the dance accelerates "till the leaves went whirling with him . . . till the dust and wind together swept in eddies round about him."

In "The Famine," Buckadawin the Famine and Ahkosewin the Fever visit Hiawatha's wigwam:

And the lovely Minnehaha
Shuddered as they looked upon her,
Shuddered at the words they uttered,
Lay down on her bed in silence,
Hid her face, but made no answer;

*The dance of Pau-Puk-Keewis as
rendered by Frederic Remington.*

Lay there trembling, freezing, burning
At the looks they cast upon her,
At the fearful words they uttered.

Hiawatha, "far away amid the forest," hears the cry
of Minnehaha:

And he rushed into the wigwam,
Saw the old Nokomis slowly
Rocking to and fro and moaning,
Saw his lovely Minnehaha
Lying dead and cold before him;
And his bursting heart within him
Uttered such a cry of anguish
That the forest moaned and shuddered,
That the very stars in heaven
Shook and trembled with his anguish.

With the assistance of Jeannette Thurber,
Dvořák sought to find or commission an English-
language libretto for his *Hiawatha* opera. Though he
began work on the music, no adequate text ever
materialized. But some of Dvořák's *Hiawatha*
sketches made their way into the symphony that
would become his most beloved composition.

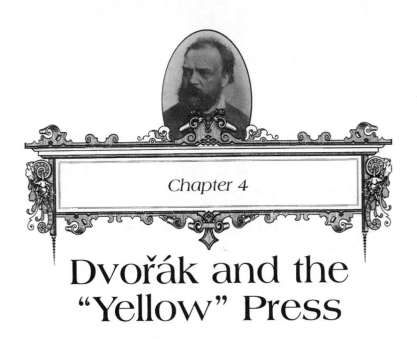

Chapter 4

Dvořák and the "Yellow" Press

**REAL VALUE OF
NEGRO MELODIES.**

Dr. Dvorak Finds In Them the
Basis for an American
School of Music.

RICH IN UNDEVELOPED THEMES.

American Composers Urged to Study
Plantation Songs and Build
Upon Them.

USES OF NEGRO MINSTRELSY.

Colored Students To Be Admitted to the National Conservatory — Prizes to Encourage Americans

The great Bohemian composer Dr. Antonín Dvořák has just ended his first season of musical exploration in New York and his opinion ought to stir the heart of every American who loves music.

"I am now satisfied," he said to me, "that the future music of this country must be founded upon what are called the Negro melodies. This must be the real foundation of any serious and original school of composition to be developed in the United States. When I first came here last year I was impressed with this idea and it has developed into a settled conviction. These beautiful and varied themes are the product of the soil. They are American. I would like to trace out the traditional authorship of the Negro melodies, for it would throw a great deal of light upon the question I am most deeply interested in at present.

"These are the folk songs of America and your composers must turn to them. All of the real musicians have borrowed from the songs of the common people. I myself have gone to the simple, half forgotten tunes of the Bohemian peasants for hints in my most serious work. Only in this way can a musician express the true sentiment of his people. He gets into touch with the common humanity of his country.

"In the Negro melodies of America I discover all that is needed for a great and noble school of music. They are pathetic, tender, passionate, melancholy, solemn, religious, bold, merry, gay or what you will. It is music that suits itself to any mood or any purpose. There is nothing in the whole range of composition that cannot be supplied with themes from this source."

And saying so Dvořák sat down at his piano and ran his fingers lightly over the keys. It was his favorite pupil's adaptation of a Southern melody.

This leads to an important announcement that the Herald is authorized to make today, which is that the National Conservatory of Music, over which Dr. Dvořák presides, is to be thrown open free of charge to the Negro race. The importance of this step can only be appreciated in the light of Dr. Dvořák's declaration that Negro melody furnishes the only sure base for an American school of music.

This institution has determined to add to the 800 white students as many Negroes of positive talent as may apply. There will be absolutely no limit. I have the authority of Mrs. Thurber herself for that.

D vořák's insistence that the "future music" of the United States be founded upon "Negro melodies," as quoted in the *Herald* on May 21, 1893, was the most famous, influential, and controversial sentence he ever uttered. But he neither said nor wrote exactly what the *Herald* printed. And the impact of his words partly depended on behind-the-scenes plotting.

Shortly before leaving America, Dvořák coauthored a magazine article in which he said, "An American reporter once told me that the most valuable talent a journalist could possess is a 'nose for news.' Just so the musician must prick his ear for music. Nothing must be too low or too insignificant for the musician." Dvořák's ear heard plantation song and minstrel tunes. The nose of James Creelman scented news. As Jeannette Thurber's ace publicist, he was as crucial an ingredient in Dvořák's campaign for Negro

James Creelman.

melodies as Harry Burleigh, Stephen Foster, or Henry Krehbiel.

Creelman was a major player in the New York newspaper wars of the day. As of 1890, New York City had forty-three daily papers. Joseph Pulitzer's *World* and William Randolph Hearst's *Journal*, competing for readers, vied for the most spectacular stories. The peculiar intensity of American journalism was experienced by all famous visitors, besieged by aggressive reporters in hot pursuit of an exclusive "scoop." Dvořák, writing home, marveled at the American addiction to "sensational gossip."

A special newspaper weapon of the late nineteenth century was "yellow journalism." Known as "the journalism that acts," it contradicted the emphasis on "facts" that respectable newspapers like the *New York Times* had begun to uphold. The term derived from the Yellow Kid, a maniacal comic strip character who could be relied upon to create mayhem wherever he appeared. Yellow journalists might feign insanity in order to expose conditions in an asylum for the poor or solve a murder by scrutinizing corpses in a morgue. But by far the biggest and most notorious of all yellow journalism stories was the Spanish-American War of 1898, which began when the United States battleship Maine exploded in Havana harbor. Though the cause of the explosion was never determined, the yellow press blamed Spain, of which Cuba was then a colony. Crying "Remember the *Maine!*" the *World* and *Journal* inflamed public opinion in support of war with such hysterical (and inaccurate) headlines as:

WAR! SURE!

MAINE DESTROYED BY SPANISH

THIS PROVED ABSOLUTELY BY DISCOVERY OF TORPEDO HOLE!

During the short war that duly followed, American correspondents traveled with the rebel Cuban troops, sleeping on the ground, eating horse meat, and carrying guns. On one occasion, *Journal* reporters freed an imprisoned "Cuban girl martyr" by suspending a wooden plank between a prison cell window and a rooftop thirty-five feet above street level. Creelman, who vowed to help the Cuban cause even it if meant "shedding blood," took part in charging a Spanish fort—and was shot in the back. Before being taken to a hospital, he was visited in the field by Hearst himself, who (as reported by Creelman) said, "I'm sorry you're hurt. But wasn't it a splendid fight? We beat every paper in the world!" On another occasion, Hearst said of Creelman, "Whatever you give him to do instantly becomes in his mind the most important assignment ever given any writer."

Creelman's specialties included getting famous people to say famous things. He paddled up the Missouri River to talk to Sitting Bull, got the Russian novelist Leo Tolstoy to express his controversial views on marriage, and obtained a rare interview with Pope Leo XIII, whom he lectured on Protestant-Catholic relations. He was said to have inflicted "cardiac spasms" on King George of Greece, who vowed never again to talk with an American journalist. His technique was to disdain taking notes while engaged in conversation, and only later to set down the "notable and striking things" he had heard said. We may assume that when Creelman quoted someone, the wording was approximate, never exact.

During Dvořák's years in New York, Creelman was both an editor of the *Evening Telegram* and a regular contributor to its sister paper, the *Herald*. In addition, he had certain private clients, including the National Conservatory of Music. For Jeannette Thurber, his job was to get Dvořák in the papers and keep him there. In fact, the *Herald*'s unsigned article on Dvořák and "Negro melodies," quotes and all, was Creelman's work.

It was also Creelman's technique to mastermind the sequel to an exclusive "scoop." One week after "REAL VALUE OF NEGRO MELODIES," a long letter to the editor appeared in the *Herald* putting the following words (all over again) in Dvořák's mouth:

> I was deeply interested in the article in last Sunday's *Herald*, for the writer struck a note that should be sounded throughout America. It is my opinion that I find a sure foundation in the Negro melodies for a new national school of music, and my observations have already convinced me that the young musicians of this country need only intelligent direction, serious application, and a reasonable amount of public support and applause to create a new musical school in America.

To make triply sure that Dvořák's message was heeded, the letter was introduced as follows:

> Through the *Herald* today Dr. Antonín Dvořák, the foremost living composer of the world, makes an appeal for a native school of music in America that ought to awaken lovers of art from one end of the country to the other. This utterance, coming from a supreme authority, is the result of a judicial and personal examination into the musical capacity of the American people.

Meanwhile, Creelman busied himself publicizing his publicity. The European edition of the *Herald* reported Dvořák's remarks. Then, in three additional articles, leading European musicians were invited to comment on Dvořák's comments. Closer to home, the *Boston Herald* reported on AMERICAN MUSIC: DR. ANTONÍN DVOŘÁK EXPRESSES SOME RADICAL VIEWS. Next, Boston's composers, too, were asked to react. All this was duly reported in the *New York Herald* under such headlines as DVOŘÁK AWAKENS THE MUSICAL WORLD and CRITICISM OF DVOŘÁK'S THEORY. In all, the *Herald* published ten Dvořák articles in less than a month.

Of the eminent composers who were asked whether they agreed with Dvořák that plantation song would furnish America's future music, many could only express shock and incomprehension. In Vienna, Anton Bruckner said, "The basis of all music must be found in the classical works of the past. German musical literature contains no written text emanating from the Negro race, and however sweet the Negro melodies might be, they can never form the groundwork of the future music of America." It was just what Creelman wanted to hear. He had cheerfully manufactured an international musical controversy.

The crudity of the campaign dismayed Henry Krehbiel, who criticized the *Herald* in the *Tribune*. Dvořák's views dismayed James Gibbons Huneker, who carped in *The Musical Courier*. The debate over Dvořák's agenda—between the critics and Dvořák, and among the critics themselves—spiraled into high gear.

Meanwhile, Dvořák was composing his new American symphony at fever pitch—drawing on his *Hiawatha* sketches, on his impressions of New York, and on his encounters with Harry Burleigh. Though the symphony was not a narrative, its points of inspiration included the wooing of Minnehaha, the dance of Pau-Puk-Keewis, Minnehaha's death, the defeat of Pau-Puk-Keewis, and Hiawatha's departure to the hereafter.

The music was equally saturated with the influence of plantation song. The first movement nearly quoted "Swing Low, Sweet Chariot." The theme of the slow movement, a hymn, shared the yearning tone of "Deep River." It would become the most famous tune Dvořák ever composed. He instantly shared it with his students, playing and singing it— wordlessly, but with such fervor that his eyes bulged and the veins of his neck turned purple, his whole body vibrating with religious feeling.

Dvořák's modest workload at the conservatory facilitated rapid progress. He had already written to friends:

My dear Doctor Kozánek,
I am as fit as a fiddle and in good heart and very well off. Boys in the street and drunk Irish

women, these are the things that annoy me, but one gets accustomed to everything.

There is one young man named Maurice Arnold upon whom I am building strong expectations. His compositions are based upon Negro melodies, and I have encouraged him in this direction. The other members of the composition class seem to think that it is not in good taste to get ideas from the old plantation songs, but they are wrong, and I have tried to impress upon their minds the fact that the greatest composers have not considered it beneath their dignity to go to the humble folk songs for motifs.

Of the critics, some are against me, but the others are good friends and write fairly and sometimes enthusiastically. I should like to have still more enemies than I have in Vienna. I have a good disposition; I can stand a lot and still be quite ready to forgive them. I sit firmly in the saddle and I like it here.

In fact, my wish to return to Bohemia will not be realized this year; we have decided otherwise. As you know, only two of the children are with us in America. Now the other four, and also my sister-in-law, Mrs. Koutecka, are coming. They will leave Prague on May 23, taking the Havel from Bremen via Southampton in England. God grant, on May 31 I shall look upon the faces of my dear and long-missed Anna, Magda, Ottie, and Zinda. Then we spend our summer in the State of Iowa,

*in the Czech village of Spillville where the teacher
and the parish priest and everything are Czech. So
I shall be among my own folks.*

*The music teacher there, Mr. Kovařík, is the
father of my assistant. The priest, Father Bily, is
a very lively fellow, so they say. He has two pairs
of ponies, and we shall ride to Protivin, a little
town nearby. In America there are names of towns
and villages of all nations under the sun!*

*Iowa is 1,300 miles from New York, but here
such a distance is nothing. It is farther than from
where you are to London.*

*I am now just finishing my E minor Symphony.
I take great pleasure in it. It will differ very considerably from my others. Well, the influence of
America must be felt by everyone who has any
"nose" at all.*

More another time.

With affectionate greetings to you and to all,

Antonín Dvořák

The final page of the symphony *From the New
World* is inscribed: "Praise God! Completed 24 May
1893 at 9 o'clock in the morning. The children have
arrived at Southampton."

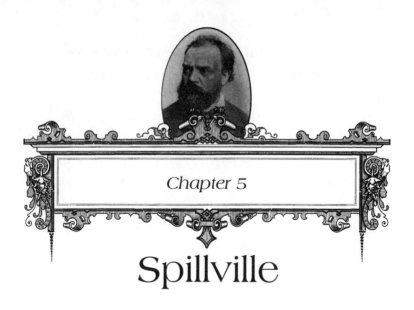

Chapter 5

Spillville

Spillville, Iowa, was named after its first settler: Joseph Spielman, who arrived in 1854 to lay claim to a picturesque valley site. The land had been vacated by Indians—Sioux, Sauk, Winnebago, and Fox—chased north and west by an 1838 treaty with the United States government. Entitled to "squatter's rights," more than 300,000 Bohemian peasants moved into Iowa, Minnesota, Wisconsin, Illinois, and Nebraska by 1890.

Spillville's 400 inhabitants were mainly Bohemian farmers. The local landmark, surrounded by red rooftops, was a substantial church: St. Wenceslaus, begun in 1850. By 1885, the bell tower featured an impressive four-face clock. Main Street, though unpaved, was lit by kerosene lamps and fringed with brick sidewalks.

Dvořák and his entourage—Anna Dvořák, the six children, Aunt Terezie, her servant, and Josef Kovařík—arrived the morning of June 5, 1893. They had begun their journey two days before at the Pennsylvania Railroad Harbor Terminal in New Jersey, a station even larger than New York's Grand Central Depot. The Chicago Express, which Dvořák and Kovařík had often observed from their West 155th Street lookout, was their train. It took the Dvořák party as far as MacGregor, Iowa, where they transferred to a branch line. At Calmar, they were welcomed by Kovařík's father, Jan, and two local priests. A pair of horse-drawn buggies conveyed

St. Wenceslaus Church.

Interior of St. Wenceslaus Church.

them the remaining five miles to Spillville. There they were taken to the brick house of Jacob Schmidt. They would occupy the upper floor for the summer.

Dvořák arose at five the next morning. The birds, the barking dogs, the fragrant soil, the blue islands of wild aster—everything made him feel at home as he never could in New York or even Prague. He quickly established a daily routine. He would take his early morning walk at four, often along the thickly forested banks of the Turkey River. Beginning around five, he would work at home, using a little pump organ. Its two foot pedals were depressed in alternation to activate the sound. At seven, he played the pipe organ at St. Wenceslaus for morning Mass. He then returned home to compose some more. Lunch consisted of rye bread and beer. For his second daily constitutional, he would get a pail of beer at a local tavern. (Though Spillville was officially "dry," it smuggled beer from nearby Decorah.) In the late afternoon he liked to chat with the older settlers at Joe Kapino's or Caspar Benesh's saloon. After dinner, he would play cards and make music at the Kovaříks'—who possessed Spillville's only piano.

In New York, Dvořák succumbed to "nerve storms" and required constant companionship. He seemed withdrawn. In Spillville, there were no students, no millionaires, no critics, no concerts, no crowds. He did not feel the "American push." And there were musical traditions, Bohemian traditions, not to be found in Manhattan. No public gathering—no wedding, funeral, or holiday; no ball or pigeon shoot—was complete without music and dance. The church choir and village band, both under Kovařík's direction, were as essential to daily life as food (or, as in Dvořák's case, drink).

In the course of the summer, Dvořák visited with Czech Americans in Omaha and St. Paul. In Chicago, he took part in Czech Day at the World Columbian Exposition. And Spillville had its own visitors: the Kickapoo Medicine Show, a troupe of professional Native American entertainers that furnished Dvořák with his best opportunity to observe and interact with actual Native Americans.

The traveling medicine show was then in its heyday. With 800 Indian performers, the Kickapoo show was the largest and oldest. A Kickapoo poster showed fourteen "famous medicine men," including Dr. Big Moon, who led the group (not one of whom was a Kickapoo) at Spillville. It also illustrated the packing and shipping of Native American roots, barks, and herbs used in the manufacture of such remedies as Indian Worm Killer. (In fact, all the company's products were concocted and bottled in a large plant in Connecticut.)

A typical Kickapoo "camp" consisted of ten to twenty performers. They would arrive with their own tepees and tents, plus a twenty-foot portable stage. Iowa—"where the boobs simply come up and ask to be had!" according to one pitchman—was a favorite destination. In addition to the oils and herbs the pitchmen hawked, the medicine show offered song and dance, acrobatics, and magic tricks. African American minstrels with banjo and guitar were commonly included. (By the late nineteenth century, minstrelsy included actual black performers.) The result was a chaotic New World brew: pounding tom-toms, hoarse chanting, furious ragtime dancing going all at once. Dvořák held to the seemingly curious opinion that "Indian" and "Negro" music resembled one another. As popularized in the

74   KICKAPOO INDIAN LIFE AND SCENES.

PHOTOGRAPHS OF SOME OF THE FAMOUS MEDICINE MEN ENGAGED AT THE WIGWAM.

KICKAPOO INDIAN REMEDIES

Indian Oil.

Indian Sagwa.

—INDIAN WORM KILLER—

SHIPPING THE ROOTS, BARKS, HERBS, ETC., USED IN THE
MANUFACTURE OF THE KICKAPOO REMEDIES.

Dr. POOR FOX.

Dr. BAD EAGLE.

Dr. FLOATING POPLAR.

Dr. SKY.

Dr. BIG MOON.

Dr. THUNDER.

Dr. CLEAR WATER.

Dr. EAGLE EYE.

Dr. BRAVE BEAR.

Dr. MOWRAY.

Dr. ANTELOPE.

Dr. HOLE IN THE DAY.

Dr. LONE CLOUD.

Dr. BLUE EAGLE.

KICKAPOO INDIAN OIL.—A Quick Cure for all Pains, External and Internal.

medicine show, they truly intermingled—as would jazz, folk, and rock styles in the American musical melting pot of the century to come.

In Spillville, where the Kickapoo Medicine Show performed nightly for more than two weeks, Big Moon became a local favorite. For the Spillville children, he crafted arrows as long as five feet and shot them phenomenal distances. Dvořák never missed a Kickapoo performance. He took a special interest in the minstrels' rendition of Stephen Foster's "Old Folks at Home," a song he already adored. He several times invited the Native Americans to a local inn to better observe their customs and songs. He tried Kickapoo Indian Oil ("A Quick Cure for all Pains, External and Internal") for a headache and exclaimed: "Pálí to jako hrom!" ("It burns like thunder!")

The young people of Spillville had their own Dvořák stories. For bird-watching purposes, he liked to sit on the stump of a great white oak split by lightning. He would have the children chase blue jays into the air in order to notate their songs. When he ran out of paper, he would write on his shirt cuffs. He would join them in treks along the Turkey River or (if they agreed to bait his hook) fishing at Jacob Schmidt's farm—only to suddenly announce that everyone had to return home "because my cuffs are already full of notes." The village laundress had a tough time cleaning his shirts.

Dear Friend,

Our three months in Spillville will remain a happy memory for the rest of our lives. Though we find the heat rather trying, it gives us great joy to be among our Czech countrymen. Imagine, after eight months in America I heard again the singing of birds! And here the birds are different from ours, they have much brighter colors and sing differently, too.

Spillville is a purely Czech settlement. Children go to an American school, but they are still Czechs. Some of the old people can speak nothing but Czech, but the younger ones, most of whom have grown up in America, speak English as well as Americans do. The children, I have noticed, speak nothing else, although they can answer in Bohemian when spoken to.

These people—all the poorest of the poor— came about forty years ago, mostly from the neighborhood of Pisek, Tabor, and Budejovice. And after great hardships and struggle, they are very well off here. I like to hear stories about the harshness of the early winters and the building of the railroad. They are all fond of me, especially the grandmas and granddads when I play in church "Go Before Thy Majesty" and "A Thousand Times We Greet Thee." Before I came, everyone was accustomed to "silent Mass," undisturbed by the organ and singing. Now they come up to say: "Mr.

Spillville.

Dvořák, the singing was fine today," or "What hymns will you be playing us tomorrow?"

With Father Bily we often go to visit Czech farmers four and five miles away. It is very strange. Few people and a great deal of empty space. A farmer's nearest neighbor is often four miles off. Especially in the prairies (I call them the Sahara), there are only endless acres of field and meadow and that is all. You are glad to see in the woods and meadows the huge herds of cattle which, summer and winter, are out to pasture in the broad fields. And so it is very "wild" here and sometimes very sad—sad to despair. But habit is everything.

We have recently come back from Chicago where, as you probably know, the twelfth of August was "Czech Day" at the Columbian Exhibition being held in celebration of the discovery of America

The house in which Dvořák lived (left).

only 400 years ago. There were about 30,000 American Czechs in procession and a concert in the big Festival Hall (orchestra of 114 performers, audience of 8,000). I conducted my own compositions, and Mr. Hlavac from Russia conducted other works by Czech composers. The orchestra was splendid and the excitement general. All the papers wrote enthusiastically, as you will probably learn from your own papers. Also, the Chicago Tribune *printed a long article about my work in America—all supposedly in my words and more or less correct.*

The exhibition itself is gigantic. It must be seen and seen very often, and still you do not really know anything. There is so much, and everything is so big, so truly "made in America."

I hope very much that I shall be able to pay a visit home to Bohemia, even if my contract in New York is prolonged. I must see Bohemia, no matter what. I hear the papers at home are writing as if I wished to stay in America for good! Oh, no— never! But God be praised, I am in good health and am working well. I know that, as for my new symphony, string quartet, and quintet, I should never have written these works "just so" if I hadn't seen America. You will no doubt hear them soon, after their performances in New York.

With affectionate greetings,

Yours,

D vořák's most memorable summertime trip took him to St. Paul, Minnesota, at the invitation of Father Jan Rynda, whom he had met in Chicago. Father Rynda hosted a banquet in Dvořák's honor for 3,000 local Czech Americans. But what made St. Paul memorable was an eager side trip to Minnehaha Falls—after which Hiawatha's wife is named, in Longfellow's poem, by her father, the Arrow Maker:

Wayward as the Minnehaha,
With her moods of shade and sunshine,
Eyes that smiled and frowned alternate
Feet as rapid as the river
Tresses flowing like the water,
And as musical as laughter;
And he named her for the river,
For the waterfall he named her,
Minnehaha, Laughing Water.

Dvořák found the fifty-three-foot waterfall bewitching in its evocation of Longfellow's poem—and scribbled a theme on his shirt cuff. Upon returning to New York in September with his family and Kovařík, he composed a little Sonatina for violin and piano. He dedicated it to his children, who took turns giving the first performances at home on East Seventeenth Street. He told his publisher that the Sonatina was intended for children "but was also suitable for adults."

The Minnehaha theme Dvořák set down on his shirt sleeve found its way into the second movement of the Sonatina, a delicate and fragrant Hiawatha picture. Its simplicity, its tom-tom repetitions, its aura of magic and mystery would typify Dvořák's "Indian" style. Minnehaha's "wayward" alternation between "shade and sunshine" translated into a musical alternation between the brighter and darker keys composers call "major" and "minor." In the middle of the movement, a dainty two-note violin figure dappled shimmering chords high in the keyboard (Minnehaha Falls being no Niagara): truly, the music of "Laughing Water."

The Violin Sonatina was Dvořák's final souvenir of his Iowa summer. Earlier, in Spillville, he had composed a quintet for strings, a suite for piano, and a string quartet—all of which (as he himself remarked) conveyed an American accent. Like a Bohemian painter rendering the landscapes and moods of a fascinating foreign land, he evoked the American West with a genius no native artist could match.

All Dvořák's Spillville compositions mirrored his summertime happiness and relaxation. The *New World* Symphony, for an orchestra of a hundred, was a New York work, full of high drama and driving energy. His Iowa music was intimate. The five players in the quintet—two violinists, two violists, and a cellist—charmingly suggested the drumbeat rhythms of the Kickapoo performers. The *American* Suite, for solo piano, featured an *Allegretto* as distant from the *Slavonic Dances* of Dvořák's youth as blackface is from the peasantry of Europe. Only high-stepping, hand-waving American minstrels could have inspired the happy-go-lucky first theme. The leaping, striding left hand of the pianist forecast Scott Joplin and his *Maple Leaf Rag* of 1899. The same piano suite featured a spacious slow movement inspired by the vast and unpopulated Iowa prairie, and a pounding "Indian" finale suitable for tom-tom accompaniment.

By far the most famous of Dvořák's Spillville compositions, however, was the *American* String Quartet. Amazingly, Dvořák sketched all twenty-five minutes in only three days during his first week in Iowa. Rejoining his family in a rural paradise, he composed music bustling with barely controlled excitement in the face of fresh experience and a new environment.

Something of Spillville became audible on the quartet's every page. The opening measures, with their quivering accompaniment, registered a fresh morning breeze. "How beautifully the sun shines!" wrote Dvořák upon finishing this first movement. The plaintive song of the slow second movement echoed in a vast natural space—broad New World horizons, New World terrain flat as far as the eye could see. As Dvořák had written, "It is sometimes very sad—sad to despair." The short third movement was a snapshot of village merriment "at the inn," punctuated by Turkey River bird calls high on the violin. The skipping rhythm of the finale suggested the *click-clack* of the Chicago Express, on which the Dvořáks had journeyed only days before, the wide western landscape whipping past, the family cheerfully reunited and breathless with anticipation.

The first performance of the *American* String Quartet took place at Kovařík's house. Dvořák and Jan Kovařík were the violinists; Kovařík's daughter played the cello; Josef Kovařík, the viola. The good fortune of this remote Iowa family was equaled only by Dvořák's good fortune, rescued from city life, whether of the New World or the Old.

Dvořák was not the only famous European composer to come to America. But compared to the others— to Igor Stravinsky, Arnold Schoenberg, or Paul Hindemith, all of whom would stay longer—only Dvořák acquired a distinct American accent. Possessed of traditions older than America itself, he never considered himself culturally superior. His eagerness to sample the sights and sounds of the New World was memorably documented in his music. His Americanization made him both instantly popular and—as the *New World* Symphony would show—instantly controversial.

Upon returning to New York from Iowa, Dvořák confided to Josef Kovařík, "Spillville is an ideal place; I would like to spend the rest of my days there." Kovařík himself wrote, in his memoirs, that the three months in Spillville were the happiest period of Dvořák's life.

Chapter 6

The *New World* Symphony

Dvořák and Seidl were sitting opposite one another at the second-floor round table of Fleischmann's Café. Both were puffing big cigars. Seidl's black suit complemented his glossy black hair, combed straight back from the forehead. His dark eyes surveyed the ceiling from behind spectacles. His sculpted features and puckered lips conveyed an air of thoughtfulness. Dvořák's bulldog face and bristling red beard were as rude as the four big beer tankards that stood empty before him. The room smelled of smoke.

In between silences, a familiar topic was addressed. "The musical life of this country is in the hands of foreigners," Dvořák muttered. "All the composers sound German."

97

Seidl stared at the table and said, "There is Victor Herbert. There is Edward MacDowell. They have a future."

"And they have a past. They studied in Stuttgart and Frankfurt. They made their reputations in Germany."

"You should not underestimate the energy of Americans. I am here longer than you. Look at the ladies of the Seidl Society, what they have done on Coney Island: my summer concerts there, fourteen times a week, for twenty-five cents a ticket. Never could you find such a thing in the Old World. And the ladies of the society don't work for money. They raise the money to create concerts for the working man."

"Yes, the women here are different. Mrs. Thurber—certainly there is no one like her in Prague or Vienna. Maybe my new symphony . . ."

"But you are not American. Incidentally, I have been looking at your new symphony. The second movement."

Dvořák bristled.

"It is a slow movement, *nein?*" said Seidl.

Dvořák exhaled a gust of cigar smoke.

"Andante, you call it," Seidl continued in his low, steady voice. "But I am sure that it is slower. A Largo. That is to get underneath, to the inner meaning. The *Innigkeit.*"

Dvořák was now talking to himself: "But of course it is an Andante. The tempo is only moderately

Anton Seidl.

slow. It is like a slave song sung by Burleigh, like 'Deep River.' "

Dvořák confronted Seidl's gaze. "No one can sing so slowly." he said. "Burleigh . . ."

"*Ja! Ja!* Burleigh!" Seidl snorted and glanced away. "This is not Burleigh. This is *Heimweh—*

homesickness. Your 'New World' Symphony is an 'Old World' Symphony. Negro music, Indian music, it is all very fine. It is what the Americans call window dressing. It is not the heart of this music. Your heart—is it in New York? Or in Bohemia?"

Seidl pointed at his chest. Dvořák ordered another Pilsner. Minutes passed.

"Do as you please," said Dvořák.

Seidl lifted his watch from his pocket. "I must rehearse," he said, and left the table.

Speaking with Seidl was one thing. But Dvořák had never had to answer so many questions. Jeannette Thurber wanted to know if the new symphony would be a model for her student composers. Creelman was always putting words into his mouth: What were the Negro melodies? How many did he use? Wasn't it really an "American" symphony after all? Fat Jim Huneker didn't think so; he was spreading rumors that the symphony had been composed in Prague. Henry Krehbiel, even fatter—how huge these Americans were! and how nosy—Krehbiel had called three times to copy down themes from the symphony and discuss their "American traits." And here, in the morning *Daily Tribune*, was an article by Krehbiel so hideously long it could not be read to the end. But everyone knew what it said anyway.

The production of a new symphony by the eminent Bohemian composer would be a matter of profound

> interest under any circumstances, but on this occasion is
> given a unique and special value by the fact that in the
> new work Dr. Dvořák has exemplified his theories touching
> the possibility of founding a national school of composi-
> tion on the folk song of America.

God! Even an American would have trouble wading through such thick prose!

Dvorak sometimes felt like a man in borrowed clothes, masquerading as a Negro, or an Indian. But he was a Bohemian—in American garb. Maybe Seidl was right. Maybe Huneker was right! He had decided to skip yesterday's public rehearsal. But tonight's concert was unavoidable: the formal premiere, with Seidl conducting the New York Philharmonic at Carnegie Music Hall. He had even trimmed his beard for the occasion. The three older children were going.

"Ottie! Aloisia! Maggie! Anna, where are the girls?"

"Any moment, Papa!"

"But the carriage is waiting."

The December night was cold and clear. As always after dark, Fifth Avenue was glamorous and aloof: the huge Gothic mansions of Vanderbilt Row, with their fairy-tale gables and turrets, approached. Dvořák told the driver to turn west and go up Sixth Avenue instead.

The entrance to Carnegie Hall was clogged. Top hats, walking sticks, monocles; pearls and evening gowns. Dvořák groaned. The bodies parted as the family stepped onto the curb. Ladies and gentlemen bowed elaborately in greeting. The Dvořáks strode briskly—too briskly—into the huge red auditorium and up four flights of stairs to a box. Jeannette and Francis Thurber were there, along with Creelman. Dvořák noticed Joseffy nearby. And his students: Arnold, Loomis, Strothotte, Shelley, Goldmark. In truth, all of musical New York was present.

The orchestra tuned. The packed hall fell silent. Seidl entered and permitted himself the merest of bows. Then he turned to his men and raised his baton.

Carnegie Music Hall.

Carnegie Hall as Dvořák knew it: entrance, lobby, auditorium.

Dvořák could not concentrate on the Mendelssohn overture. The second number, the Violin Concerto his friend Brahms had composed fifteen years before, distracted him for a time. How padded and "learned" it sounded. It reminded him of Krehbiel's articles—awful thought. Even the Gypsy dance in the last movement was Viennese café music—nothing like Big Moon and Iowa, or Burleigh singing "Deep River," nothing like his own new symphony.

Intermission. Impossible to pace the lobby. Trapped.

Finally, the main event: *Z Novecho Sveta*, "From the New World." Seidl's graceful upbeat—how elegantly and simply he conducted!—cued a yearning song in the cellos: a song of sorrow. Then, a vigorous tune in the horns, to an accompaniment trembling with anticipation in a proud rhythm that said, "Hi-a-wa-tha." An explosion of energy, of trumpets and trombones, with the violins sawing away furiously and the timpani pounding. Very satisfying. A sweet theme in the flute, the one suggested by "Swing Low, Sweet Chariot"—nicely done. Now taken up by the fiddles, peaches in springtime. Seidl had done his work thoroughly, lovingly. He believed in the symphony.

But he had slowed the tempo of the second movement. It had become a majestically paced Largo. The opening chorale was gravely and momentously religious; well, if it sounded like Wagner, that was

MUSIC HALL.

—

THE PHILHARMONIC SOCIETY

OF NEW YORK,

ANTON SEIDL, - - Conductor.

—

Fifty-Second Season, 1893-94.

Second Concert,

SATURDAY EVENING, DEC. 16, '93,

AT 8.15 O'CLOCK.

—

SOLOIST,

MR. HENRI MARTEAU, - - Violin.

—

PROGRAMME.

PART I.

1. OVERTURE, Scherzo, Nocturno, from
   "A Midsummer' Night's Dream," *Mendelssohn*

2. CONCERTO for Violin, in D major. op. 77,
   - - - - *Brahms*
   > *a.* Allegro non troppo, (cadenza by Henri
   > Marteau.
   > *b.* Adagio.
   > *c.* Allegro giocoso, ma non troppo vivace
   > MR. HENRI MARTEAU.

PART II.

3. SYMPHONY, "From the New World,"
   No. 5, E minor, - - - *Dvorak*
   (New; first time in America; Manuscript.)
   > I. Adagio, Allegro molto.
   > II. Larghetto.
   > III. Scherzo. Molto vivace.
   > IV. Allegro con fuoco.

105

all right. Now the English horn theme, Dvořák's favorite, the "slave song," but taken more deliberately than any human voice could sing it. Incredible. "This is not Burleigh! This is *Heimweh*." And so it was. Slowed down, the English horn song was wondrously sad. And this was not the sadness of the prairie. It was the sadness of life: Dvořák's sadness. As for the second theme—the passage for "church organ," with its steady footfall in the plucked double basses . . . Dvořák had here envisioned Minnehaha's funeral: Hiawatha and his tribesmen bearing her body on a stretcher, stoically trudging through the snow. Seidl's new tempo weighted the sadness unbearably. Dvořák discovered himself thinking of Otakar, of Josephine, of Rozaka—his three firstborn. Dead. Dead. Dead.

Anna was nudging him. He looked up and realized the hall was loud with the sound of applause. Seidl was gesturing from the podium. A reflex action caused Dvořák's legs to straighten and his body to rise. Looking down, looking to either side, looking up, he encountered 2,500 faces fixed on his own. "Dvořák!" "Dvořák!" With trembling hands—even his legs were trembling—he motioned to Seidl, to the orchestra, to the audience. He touched his cheek and discovered it was moist.

The commotion subsided as suddenly as it had begun. (Symphonies are not normally interrupted by applause midway through.) The exuberant third movement was a relief. Tom-toms and a skittish dance, rapidly gathering momentum: Pau-Puk-Keewis, the dandy, at Hiawatha's wedding:

> First he danced a solemn measure
> Treading softly like a panther
> Then more swiftly and still swifter,
> Whirling, spinning round in circles,
> Leaping o'er the guests assembled,
> Eddying round and round the wigwam,
> Till the leaves went whirling with him,
> Stamped upon the sand and tossed it
> Wildly in the air around him.

Or was it the whirling of short skirts: a Czech *furiant*? Well, yes and no. But the lilting waltz tune later in the movement—that was Bohemian, sure enough, a rustic wedding. And the proud, angry finale? Hiawatha music:

> Full of wrath was Hiawatha
> When he came into the village,
> Found the people in confusion,
> Heard of all the misdemeanours,
> All the malice and mischief
> Of the cunning Pau-Puk-Keewis.

> Hard his breath came through his nostrils,
> Through his teeth he buzzed and muttered
> Words of anger and resentment,
> Hot and humming, like a hornet.

The death of Minne-
haha as rendered by
Frederic Remington.

"I will slay this Pau-Puk-Keewis,
Slay this mischief-maker!" said he.
"Not so long and wide the world is
Not so rude and rough the way is,
That my wrath shall not attain him,
That my vengeance shall not reach him!"

In the closing moments of the symphony, the jagged theme of Hiawatha's wrath was broadened and transformed into a weighty dirge in the trumpets, with Hiawatha's first movement theme superimposed in horns and trombones: Hiawatha's leave-taking "in the glory of the sunset." A noble requiem.

The shouting and stamping that erupted at the conclusion of the *New World* Symphony was not like the sound of ovations in European halls. Even Seidl was clapping. Members of the orchestra waved their instruments. A half-dozen critics mobbed Dvořák's box, competing to be the first to congratulate him. Dvořák acknowledged it all, left the box, and put on his coat. He ventured into the lobby with Anna and the children—and found it nearly empty. Inside the auditorium, the ovation continued. And so Dvořák returned to the railing and doffed his top hat until everyone was satisfied that the evening was over. On the street he wiped his brow and remarked to Creelman, ever at his heels: "He who will, can. He who can, must."

Of the newspaper reviews the next morning, Dvořák's favorite was W. J. Henderson's, in the *Times*. He even read parts of it aloud to Anna and the girls: "We are inclined to regard it as the best of Dr. Dvořák's works in this form, which is equivalent to saying that it is a great symphony and must take its place among the finest works in the form produced since the death of Beethoven."

Henderson's was the longest concert review Dvořák had ever seen—even longer than one of Krehbiel's. It began by considering the meaning of the title, *From the New World*. Dvořák came to America as a teacher, Henderson explained. He understood that there existed no symphonies or operas that sounded "American." This was caused by a failure to identify a folk music that would bind together all the country's immigrant strains—English, German, Italian. And so the music Americans composed sounded English, German, or Italian.

Dvořák decided to attempt an American symphony, Henderson continued. His intentions were misunderstood by many. They thought he would take some Civil War songs and minstrel ballads and try to make a symphony out of them. Dvořák's method, instead, was that of a master composer. Rather than quote existing folk songs, he had saturated himself with the "Negro melodies" he loved, and then invented his own themes. Similarly, he had absorbed the spirit of *The Song of Hiawatha*—a poem vast numbers of Americans identified as their own.

Henderson's review reached a peak of eloquence, where he asked of the *New World* Symphony: "Is it American?" Dvořák's critics had contended that the slave songs were not the songs of America, and may not even have been created by slaves. Henderson retorted that whatever their point of origin—whether in Africa or Mississippi, whether white or black—

111

such songs as "Deep River" and "Swing Low" emerged in the American South, influenced by the plantation system and its cruel conditions. The tunefulness and sincerity of the slave songs "struck an answering note in the American heart." They inspired the most popular of all American composers—Stephen Foster.

> The American people—or the majority of them—learned to love the songs of the negro slave and to find in them something that belonged to America. If those songs are not national, then there is no such thing as national music.

"That's it!" cried Dvořák, slapping the table. Anna and the children were startled.

"What's 'it,' Ton?" Anna asked.

"Bill Henderson says it right here—that Negro music is American music. And listen to this! 'A national song is one that is of the people, for the people, by the people. The Negroes gave us this music, and we accepted it.' Using Abraham Lincoln's words!"

"Abraham who?"

Dvořák dropped the newspaper and left the house for a walk around Stuyvesant Park. Yes, Seidl was right: there was emptiness and despair in the *New World* Symphony. Henderson was right: the symphony was full of first American impressions—a picturesque outer layer of Indians and plantation song. And it all fit together. Indians and slaves were outcasts in America, victims of a tragic fate. Their suffering, their fortitude, inspired sorrow, compassion, and admiration.

"I was raised in an atmosphere of struggle and endeavor," Dvořák had said over and again. Struggle and endeavor. That was man's condition on Earth. It was universal. A musician's job was to dig deep enough to find a common humanity before God.

Dvořák felt wonderfully fulfilled.

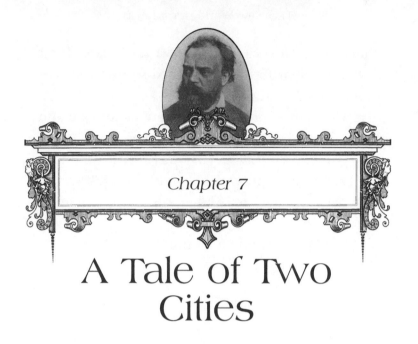

Chapter 7

A Tale of Two Cities

Two weeks after the triumphant premiere of the *New World* Symphony in New York, Henry Krehbiel entered Symphony Hall to review the first Boston performance. This was enemy territory: Boston and New York were keen rivals for American musical supremacy. Normally, Krehbiel assessed the state of the Boston Symphony during its annual visits to Carnegie Music Hall. But on special occasions he ventured to the orchestra's home base, there to joust with Philip Hale of the *Home Journal*. The two critics were as different as the two cities.

Boston had already made its Dvořák views known. Krehbiel had read with exasperation the comments of Boston's composers, as elicited by James Creelman.

Henry Krehbiel.

"Such Negro melodies as I have heard I should be sorry to see become the basis of an American school of musical composition," George Chadwick had declared. Amy Beach said, "Without the slightest desire to question the beauty of the Negro melodies of which Dvořák speaks so highly, or to disparage them on account of their source, I cannot help feeling justified in the belief that they are not fully typical of our country. The African population of the United States is far too small for its songs to be considered 'American.'"

115

Even more irritating, in Krehbiel's view, had been the response when Dvořák himself came to Boston a year before to conduct his *Requiem*. Imagine denouncing such a refined work as "barbarous"! This was Boston shorthand for "Slavic" or "non-German." The *Boston News* added: "After his visit to Boston Dr. Dvořák will probably find it even harder to take up his residency permanently in New York."

As Krehbiel appreciated all too well, Boston saw itself as a haven of intellectual repose, of hallowed traditions preserved by its oldest and "best" families. There was something to this, of course. Lower Manhattan, teeming with immigrants to the east, with German saloons and theaters to the west, had no Boston equivalent. New York was crowded, concrete, and loud. Boston was green and sedate. New York had no writers comparable to Ralph Waldo Emerson, Henry David Thoreau, or Nathaniel Hawthorne—all of them steeped in New England nature, lore, and religion. And the Boston Symphony Orchestra, founded in 1881 by Henry Higginson, was certainly America's finest.

Higginson's musical taste, formed in Vienna, was Germanic; French, Italian, and Russian composers were second-best to Bach, Mozart, Beethoven, and Schubert. In fact, the Boston view of Dvořák was essentially Vienna's or Berlin's: that he was a peasant of genius, a sublime simpleton. Insofar as he advocated an American school, he was also an unwanted visitor—unlike New York, Boston already had a composers' community of its own. Worse yet, Dvořák was linked to New York and its immigrant melee, teeming with Slavs, Jews, and every other ethnic strain. Surely he was, as Hale once put it, "stupefied" by Manhattan's "din and bustle."

And here came Philip Hale himself, ever dapper, courtly, and trim, taking his accustomed seat on the aisle. Krehbiel fondly fingered his enormous paunch. How had Shakespeare put it? "Yon Cassius has a lean and hungry look—such men are dangerous." Trust a fat man every time.

A privileged member of the Boston elite, Hale was eighth in line of descent from Thomas Hale, who settled in Massachusetts in the early seventeenth century. He had attended Phillips Exeter Academy, where he had a private tutor, then Yale University, after which he had studied in Paris. Krehbiel was a self-made American. The son of German immigrants, born in Cincinnati, he had been a teenage newspaper reporter before becoming a critic. He had never attended college, but he was a prodigious learner. When he approvingly cited Dvořák's faith in the poor ("They work hard, they study seriously"), he wrote from personal experience.

Listening to the Boston orchestra perform Dvořák, Krehbiel was sensitive to every defect. To be sure, this was a more polished group than Seidl's New York Philharmonic (which could afford to perform only twelve times a year). And Boston's audience was quieter and more reverent than the Carnegie crowd. Too reverent—Krehbiel's spine tingled recalling how in New York the symphony had been interrupted with wild applause and cheering halfway through. Symphony Hall itself, so plain and wooden, looked like a church. As for Emil Paur, the Boston conductor—now *there* was a true barbarian! He wasn't fit to tune Seidl's piano.

Krehbiel let Hale have the first word in the next morning's *Journal*. Hale liked the *New World* Symphony. How could he not? But while he conceded that "Negro airs" might "tint slightly two or three passages," he insisted that the symphony's success was unrelated to anything "American"; it equally sounded Scottish or Scandinavian or "anything you please." In fact, Hale believed that "the Negro is not inherently musical," that his plantation songs were borrowed from white singers, and that in any case, they were no more American than were "the tunes of the aboriginal Indians." He ridiculed "Mr. Krehbiel" for nonetheless believing "that at last we really have a great national piece of music."

Krehbiel now wrote in the *New York Tribune*:

> Dr. Dvořák's symphony, *From the New World*, was performed in Boston on Saturday night at a concert by the Symphony Orchestra. Its success with the public, while pronounced, was not so emphatic as it was in New York, for which fact an explanation might be found in

the circumstance that it was not so well played. Mr. Paur had evidently taken ample pains in studying it with his band, but he misconceived the tempo of every movement so completely that the work was robbed of half its charm. It reminded one of the dinner at which everything was cold except the ice-cream. Every movement was played with great moderation, except the Larghetto, which was played much too fast.

The newspaper critics in their reviews are unanimous in praising the beauty of the music and denying its right to be called American. Much of this kind of talk is merely quibbling. The sarcastic and scintillant Mr. Philip Hale of *The Boston Journal* does not deny that Dr. Dvořák's melodies reflect the characteristics of the songs of the Negroes in the South, and that the symphony is beautifully and consistently made. If so, why should it not be called American? Those songs are the product of American institutions: of the social, political, and geographical environment within which the black slave was placed here; of the influences to which he was subjected here; of the joys and sorrows which fell to his lot here. They are beautiful songs, and Dr. Dvořák has showed that they can furnish symphonic material to the composer who knows how to employ it.

Hale now retorted that, based on what he had read in the New York press, the *New World* Symphony "could only be appreciated properly by an audience composed exclusively of intelligent Negroes and combed and washed Indians." He also had occasion to review the first performance of Dvořák's *American* String Quartet, which was given not in New York but in Boston, on January 1, 1894. He pronounced it

. . . on the whole, a delightful and refreshing work. The
themes are characteristic—but not necessarily or incidentally characteristic of Negro temperament, which seems
now in certain quarters to be regarded as synonymous
with American temperament. The Negroes encountered
by Mr. Dvořák have a singular habit of whistling
Bohemian tunes.

Three months later, the *American* Quintet, also a
Spillville memento, was given in Boston. One critic
wrote: "We are getting heartily tired of the uncivi-
lized in chamber and symphonic music." When, in
1896, Boston's own George Chadwick composed a
string quartet influenced by Dvořák, Hale declared
Dvořák a bad influence on American composers
and termed him a "Negrophile"—a lover of Negroes.

In truth, Dvořák was a Negrophile—and so were
Krehbiel, W. J. Henderson, Jeannette Thurber, and
scores of other Dvořák supporters in New York. No
New York critic could have written, as did William
Apthorp of the *Boston Transcript* in his *New World*
Symphony review, that

. . . the general melodic and rhythmic character of the
German, Italian, and French songs stamps them as exam-
ples of a higher stage in musical evolution. The great bane
of the present Slavic and Scandinavian Schools is and has
been the attempt to make civilized music by civilized
methods out of essentially barbaric material. Our American
Negro music has every element of barbarism to be found
in the Slavic or Scandinavian folk-songs; it is essentially

barbarous music. What is more, it sounds terribly like any other barbarous music.

The larger perspective into which this opinion fit was "Social Darwinism," which turned Charles Darwin's evolutionary theory of "survival of the fittest" into a ranking of human racial types: white "Germanic" races were at the top, with Slavs lower down, and "red" and "black" peoples at the bottom. The mixing of red or black blood with white was decried as dangerous.

In Boston, as in much of the United States, even Americans who had opposed slavery assumed the innate inferiority of black- and red-skinned human beings. Louis Agassiz of Harvard—Boston's most famous scientist—taught that blacks and whites had evolved at different rates and belonged to different species. Born in Switzerland, he first encountered blacks in Philadelphia in 1846. "I scarcely dare tell you the painful impression I received," he wrote to his sister. "As much as I try to feel pity at the sight of this degraded and degenerate race, as much as their fate fills me with compassion in thinking them as really men, it is impossible for me to repress the feeling that they are not of the same blood as us."

Dvořák, born in Bohemia, first came into contact with blacks in New York—unlike Boston, a city of immigrants, a polyglot metropolis accustomed to diversity, in which old wealth did not exert a dominant influence on musical affairs. To Dvořák (as to

Dvořák conducting.

Americans of today), Agassiz's racial theories were a product not of science, but of prejudice.

Dvořák's American presence had ignited an intense debate on the questions "Who is an American?" and "What is America?" In fact, days after the Boston Symphony first played the *New World* Symphony, Dvořák led an unusual concert at New York's Madison Square Garden—a concert unthinkable in any New England city.

The year 1893—for Dvořák, a year of public triumph in New York and private delight in Spillville— was for countless Americans a year of public turmoil and private anguish. Wall Street's Panic of 1893 bankrupted businesses, overturned personal fortunes, and left millions without work. Tramps roamed the country, begging or stealing. Armies of jobless men marched from as far away as California to petition Congress for relief. Revolution was feared or predicted. The United States government resisted playing a direct role in creating jobs or compensating the unemployed. "The results of the great industrial panic can hardly be exaggerated," commented the *New York Herald*. "Poverty on a scale never known before in this country has been forced upon multitudes of people hitherto strangers to want. What chance has a ragged man in broken shoes and a worn out hat to get a position as a bookkeeper? Feed a man and you make him comfortable. But clothe him decently and you restore his hope and self-respect."

Accordingly, James Creelman, on behalf of the *Tribune* and the National Conservatory of Music, concocted a plan that was (of course) partly public relations: a benefit concert, by the conservatory orchestra, to raise money for a clothing drive sponsored by the newspaper. Dvořák would conduct. A chorus of African American conservatory students would sing. Dvořák composed a letter of support in his faulty English. Edited by Creelman, it appeared in the *Herald* in early 1894:

> The Herald's Free Clothing Fund is the best and most practical movement that has been organized since the beginning of this terrible period of suffering. It gives every man, woman and child in this City an opportunity to do something toward clothing the hapless thousands pressing us on all sides for help. As Director of the National Conservatory of Music I am authorized to arrange and conduct a public concert in aid of this great charity. I will be most happy to do all in my power to make the concert a success.

Naturally, the fullest account of this event appeared in the *Herald* itself, written—but not signed—by James Creelman. It began:

Dvořák leads for the fund

Honor to Mrs. Jeannette M. Thurber, to Dr. Antonín Dvořák
and to the students of the National Conservatory of Music!

Thanks to their generous assistance, *The Herald*'s
Free Clothing Fund has been augmented by a donation of
$1,047. This sum represents the net proceeds of the con-
cert given last evening in Madison Square Garden Concert
Hall by the pupils of the conservatory, under the conduc-
torship of Dr. Dvořák, the director of that institution.

Success of the most pronounced kind crowned the
concert from every point of view. Long before the hour
fixed for the opening the hall was filled with an immense
throng of people. At eight o'clock there was hardly standing
room, only the aisles being kept free, and as the concert
proceeded the ranks of anxious listeners standing at the
back became more and more closely serried until they
overflowed into the passageways.

It was a unique programme. Each soloist, with one
exception, belonged to the colored race. This idea was
due to Mrs. Thurber. She threw open the doors of her
excellently equipped musical educational establishment
to pupils of ability, no matter what their race, color, or
creed. Emancipation, in her idea, had not gone far
enough. Bodies had been liberated, but the gates of the
artistic world were still locked.

Her efforts in this direction were ably seconded by Dr.
Dvořák.

However opportunistic, the concert, in the Garden's
elegant gold and white concert hall of 1,500 seats
(not its vast amphitheater, where horse shows, boxing
matches, and political rallies were held), was also
altruistic. Its novelty was genuine. Though African
American choruses were typically heard in plantation
song, the sight and sound of a symphony orchestra
assisted by 130 black singers—sopranos and altos

dressed in white, pink, or blue; tenors and basses in dark suits—was something new. Even more startling was the appearance of a black conductor—Dvořák's prize pupil, Maurice Arnold—leading white instrumentalists in his own *American Plantation Dances.* The evening's star soloist was the celebrated soprano Sissieretta Jones. Known as the "Black Patti"—a reference to Adelina Patti, then the most famous of operatic sopranos—she had at the age of twenty-four already sung for senators and chief justices, and at the White House for President Benjamin Harrison. On this occasion, singing in Latin under Dvořák's baton, she offered the "Inflammatus" from Rossini's *Stabat Mater,* a thundering prayer for salvation. In the *Herald,* Creelman reported: "Mme. Jones came in the light of revelation, singing high Cs with as little apparent effort as her namesake." She added an operatic encore in French.

In 1894, when many Americans insisted on the "innate inferiority" of the "colored races," these unusual feats by black performers in "white" music were a memorable validation of artistic competence. But the evening's star was of course Dvořák, leading his conservatory orchestra and chorus. At one point—another Creelman touch—he was presented with a gold baton "as a token of loving esteem." Crowning the entire occasion was a premiere: Dvořák had composed his own arrangement, for orchestra and chorus, of Stephen Foster's "Old Folks at Home." The soprano soloist was Sissieretta Jones. The solo baritone was twenty-eight-year-old Harry Burleigh.

Once sung with banjo by white men mimicking blacks, Foster's "Way Down upon the Swanee Ribber" was now delivered by an interracial ensemble of 180, sweetened by violins, embroidered by winds and brass, punctuated by timpani. To some, the formal dignity of Dvořák's gesture seemed naive or bizarre: a European straitjacket. And listeners a century later would dismiss Foster's 1851 song, with its carica-tured black speech, as an ugly memento of slavery.

For many blacks of Dvořák's time, however, "Old Folks at Home," once the most universally popular of all American songs, was as cherished as it was familiar. Sissieretta Jones said of it: "Is there a soul so insensible that it cannot be stirred to the very depths by the heartbroken cry of the poor old homesick darkey?" Some African Americans even claimed that Foster had stolen the tune from the plantation. Dvořák told the press that, for him, its authorship was irrelevant: "It is an American folk song and a very beautiful one, too." In any event, Dvořák's local prestige was such that his arrangement could only ennoble "Old Folks." He had musically underlined its qualities of compassion. The opening stanzas were first played by a solo flute, simply accompanied; the effect was accurately described in

Creelman's review as "desolate." At the refrain the chorus and orchestra ardently entered en masse:

> All de world am sad and dreary
> Ebry where I roam
> O! darkeys how my heart grows weary
> Far from de old folks at home!

Foster may literally have been describing a bought-and-sold slave pining for his plantation home. But for countless listeners in polyglot America, white and black, "Old Folks at Home" was about yearning and nostalgia, estrangement and exile. As in the *New World* Symphony, Dvořák's identification with an oppressed minority resonated with his own experience of displacement—especially away from home in Manhattan.

In fact, a feeling of homesickness—of *Heimweh,* as identified by Seidl in the *New World* Symphony— typified Dvořák's "American style." His craving for familiar company—of his family, of his birds, of his Czech American companions in Spillville—was an effort to make his new American environment as familiar as possible. At the same time, he reached out to this new environment in an effort to feel less estranged. It was predictable that the homeward pull to Bohemia would eventually prove stronger than the fascinations of a New World. And the social and economic turmoil of 1893 could only accelerate this homecoming.

Ironically, the National Conservatory could itself have benefited from its Madison Square Garden fundraiser: the Panic nearly bankrupted Francis Thurber, who so generously bankrolled his wife's musical philanthropies. By early 1894, Dvořák was no longer paid on schedule. Although, having summered in Bohemia, he returned to New York in October 1894 for a third term as conservatory director, his enthusiasm ebbed. The opportunity of financial security that had lured him to America evaporated; the nation itself suddenly seemed insecure. Dvořák's aversion to traffic and noise increased. He rarely went out, except to teach. He smoked more than before and was prone to depression and anxiety. In August 1895, he gently informed Jeannette Thurber—whom he now addressed in correspondence as "Dear Jeannette"—of his resignation.

Dvořák left New York having acquired a broader understanding of the New World. He was sensitized to criticism that his agenda for American music was too narrow. Though he retained his conviction that plantation song was an indispensable American folk music, he now acknowledged that America was a vibrant patchwork—a quilt of many colors—and so would be American music. His final thoughts about American music, including his continued impatience with the United States government for not supporting it, were expressed in a February 1895 article for *Harper's* magazine.

Music in America

by Antonín Dvořák

The two American traits which most impress the foreign observer, I find, are the unbounded patriotism and capacity for enthusiasm of most Americans. Unlike the inhabitants of other countries, who do not "wear their hearts upon their sleeves," the citizens of America are always patriotic, and no occasion seems to be too serious or too slight for them to give expression to this feeling. Thus nothing better pleases the average American, especially the American youth, than to be able to say that this or that building, this or that new appliance, is the finest or the grandest in the world.

This, of course, is due to that other trait—enthusiasm. The enthusiasm of most Americans for all things new is apparently without limit. It is the essence of what is called "push"——American push. Every day I meet with this quality in my pupils. They are unwilling to stop at anything. In the matters relating to their art they are inquisitive to a degree that they want to go to the bottom of all things at once. It is as if a boy wished to dive before he could swim.

At first, when my American pupils were new to me, this trait annoyed me, and I wished them to give more attention to the one matter in hand rather than to everything at once. But now I like it, for I have come to the conclusion that this youthful enthusiasm and eagerness to take up everything is the best promise for music in America.

Only when the people in general, however, begin to take as lively an interest in music and art as they now take in more material matters will the arts come into their own. Let the enthusiasm of the people once be excited, and patriotic gifts and bequests must surely follow.

It is a matter of surprise to me that all this has not come long ago. When I see how much is done in every other field by public-spirited men in America—how schools, universities, libraries, museums, hospitals, and parks spring up out of the ground and are maintained by generous gifts—I can only marvel that so little has been done for music.

Even the little republic of Switzerland annually sets aside a budget for the furtherance of literature, music and the arts.

Not long ago a young man came to me and showed me his compositions. His talent seemed so promising that I at once offered him a scholarship in our school, but he sorrowfully confessed that he could not afford to become my pupil because he had to earn his living by keeping books in Brooklyn. Even if he came just two afternoons a week, or on Saturday afternoon only, he said, he would lose his employment, on which he and others had to depend. I urged him to arrange the matter with his employer, but he only received the answer: "If you want to play, you can't keep books. You will have to drop one or the other." He dropped his music.

In any another country, the State would have made some provision for such a deserving scholar, so that he could have pursued his natural calling without having to starve. With us in Bohemia, the legislature each year votes a special sum of money for just such purposes, and the imperial government in Vienna on occasion furnishes other funds for talented artists. Had it not been for such support I should not have been able to pursue my studies when I was a young man. This has filled me with lasting gratitude toward my country.

When those who have musical talent find it worth their while to stay in America and study and exercise their art as the business of their life, the music of America will soon become more national in its character. This my conviction, I know, is not shared by many who can justly claim to know this country better than I do. Because the population of the United States is composed of many different races, and because, owing to the improved method of transmission of the present day, the music of all the world is quickly absorbed in their country, they argue that nothing specially original or national can come forth.

It is a proper question to ask, what songs, then, belong to the American and appeal more strongly to him than any others? What melody could stop him on the street if he were in a strange land and make the home feeling well up within him, no matter how hardened he might be or how wretchedly the tune were played? Their number, to be sure, seems to be limited. The most potent as well as the most beautiful among them, according to my estimation, are certain of the so-called plantation melodies and slave songs. I, for one, am delighted by them. But it matters little whether the inspiration for the coming folk songs of America is derived from the Negro melodies, the songs of the creoles, the red man's chant, or the plaintive ditties of the homesick German or Norwegian. Undoubtedly the germs of the best in music lie hidden among all the races that are commingled in this great country.

When music has been established as one of the reigning arts of the land, another wreath of fame and glory will be added to this country which earned the name "Land of Freedom" by unshackling her slaves at the price of her own blood.

Old
Harry Burleigh

Dvořák never returned to the United States. He died in Prague in 1904 at the age of sixty-three.

In 1922, William Arms Fisher, who had studied with Dvořák at the National Conservatory, turned the Largo of the *New World* Symphony into a slave song with the words:

Goin' home, goin' home
I'm a goin' home.
Quiet like, some still day,
I'm jes' goin' home.
It's not far, jes' close by,
Through an open door;
Work all done, care laid by,

133

Gwine to fear no more.
Mother's there 'spectin' me,
Father's waitin', too.
Lots of folk gathered there—
All the friends I knew.

So successful was this transformation that it joined the repertoire of popular spirituals—and most Americans assumed that Dvořák had quoted the noble tune, not created it. As for the *New World*, it endures to this day as the most-performed symphony composed on American soil. In fact, Dvořák's three best-known larger works—the others being the *American* String Quartet and the Cello Concerto— were composed during his American stay. Of his miniatures, the familiar G-flat Humoresque for piano is another Dvořák tune, inspired by minstrelsy and cakewalk, that many listeners mistake for an American creation.

In Dvořák's wake, hundreds of "Indianist" songs, symphonies, and even operas—many quoting actual Native American tunes—were composed in search of the American style Dvořák espoused. After 1900, Americans discovered their own "white" folk music: songs like "The Gypsy Laddie" and "The Old Chisholm Trail," found in the Appalachian Mountains or the western plains. These, too, were applied by American composers—as by Aaron Copland in *Billy the Kid* (1938). And African American song and dance continued to generate concert works and operas—of which the best-known is George Gershwin's *Porgy and Bess* (1935).

Ultimately, it was popular music that became an American specialty. Jazz, the blues, and rock influenced Europe as European music and culture had influenced the United States. And African American music and musicians were the source of these unique American sounds. Dvořák could not have foreseen jazz. But his intuition was wonderfully correct: "Negro melodies" did anchor "the future music of this country."

Of Dvořák's students at the National Conservatory, many made prominent careers in pursuit of an American musical tradition. But none achieved the fame of Harry Burleigh. When St. George's Episcopal Church, a wealthy and prestigious congregation near the conservatory, needed a baritone soloist, Jeannette Thurber recommended Burleigh, who was then considering an offer from a minstrel company. He won the audition over sixty white applicants and remained at St. George's for fifty-two years as the first African American soloist or choir member. By the 1930s, his popularity was so great that St. George's became known as "Mr. Burleigh's church," celebrated for its annual service of spirituals. The Wall Street king J. P. Morgan, a St. George's parishioner, often invited Burleigh to sing at his home. Burleigh also sang at Morgan's funeral. In fifty-two years Burleigh missed only one performance at St. George's—for his mother's funeral in 1903.

Harry Burleigh.

Meanwhile, Burleigh composed or arranged more than 150 songs. His art songs were polished in the European manner. His plantation songs were arrangements, for chorus or for voice and piano, of the slave songs. At first, the novelty of performing black songs for white audiences made some African Americans uncomfortable. Burleigh replied that such songs were "our heritage" and "ought to be preserved, studied, and idealized." In fact, the success of Burleigh's "Deep River" arrangement was such that within a year prominent vocalists, black and white, were offering it in recital alongside the classic *Lieder* of Schubert and Brahms. Burleigh set an example for Marian Anderson, Paul Robeson, and other black singers whose specialties included the slave songs he had transcribed. He had discovered a vehicle to promote "a great and noble school of music" in Dvořák's footsteps.

Burleigh was still singing and at the height of his considerable fame when the hundredth anniversary of Dvořák's birth was celebrated at Dvořák's former East Seventeenth Street home on December 13, 1941. Josef Kovařík was there, as were New York Mayor Fiorello La Guardia and New York's leading concert artists. A commemorative plaque was affixed to the house. Kovařík was too moved to speak. It was Harry Burleigh, at eighty-three still of firm voice and erect carriage, who sealed the occasion with a sermon delivered in songful pulpit tones:

"Eight decades ago, my blind grandfather taught me the songs of sorrow. I learned by listening—they were never written down. It was Dvořák who taught me that the spirituals were not meant only for the colored people, but for people of all races and of every creed.

"In New York I was with Dr. Dvořák almost constantly. He loved to hear me sing the old melodies. His humility and religious feeling—his great love for common people of all lands—enabled him to sense the pure gold of plantation song. As an outsider to our culture—as a famous and distinguished outsider, who knew and appreciated the music of the soil—he honored this music with more authority than any American could, whether black or white.

It was Dvořák who urged me to take these melodies to the world, to sing them alongside the great European art songs of Schubert, Schumann, and Brahms. If I was the first to undertake this, it was Dvořák who first instructed me to do so. He left behind an appreciation of the beauties of Negro song—of its religious atmosphere, its piquancy—from which many, many artists have since drawn solace and inspiration.

"Though I have never publicly been credited with exerting any influence on Dr. Dvořák, I suppose there isn't much doubt about it. Anyone with ears and eyes can hear and see that 'Swing Low' is the basis for one of the themes in the *New World* Symphony, which I first encountered in this very house, copying page after page as he composed it.

"I little imagined, saying good-bye in 1895, that I would never see Dr. Dvořák again—that in only ten years' time he would cross over into campground. We will remember him always as a great musician, but also for his greatness as a human being who understood, in the songs of the plantation, proof of the Negro's spiritual ascendancy over oppression and humiliation, who understood the message ever manifest: that eventual deliverance from all that hinders and oppresses the soul will come, and man—every man—will be free."

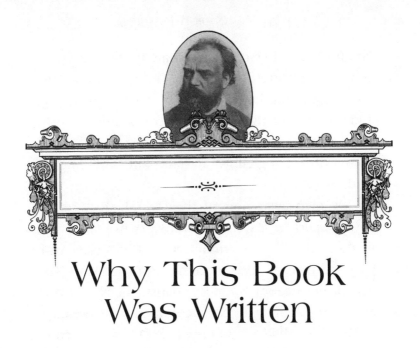

Why This Book
Was Written

There was a time when the project of introducing young Americans to "great music" mainly meant introducing a pantheon of great composers beginning with Bach, Mozart, and Beethoven. This Eurocentric curriculum seems dated today.

As a timely replacement, the story of Dvořák in America suggests itself for many reasons. No other European musician of comparable eminence so dedicated himself to finding "America." Dvořák's quest was both concentrated and varied. And he proved amazingly absorbent. In particular, his enthusiasm for the music of Native Americans and African Americans memorably bore fruit in his own symphonic, piano, and chamber works. The pedagogical

ramifications of Dvořák's quest are irresistibly multi-
cultural and interdisciplinary. The slave trade, the
Indian Wars, blackface minstrelsy, yellow journalism,
and the Panic of 1893 are among the pertinent topics.
The cast of characters includes Stephen Foster, Henry
Wadsworth Longfellow, Buffalo Bill, and Marian
Anderson.

My own awareness of the Dvořák story began
with *Wagner Nights*, my 1994 history of Wagnerism
in the United States. Immersed in 1890s New York
City culture, I also became immersed in the
American career of Wagner's charismatic New World
emissary, Anton Seidl. Seidl conducted the premiere
of the *New World* Symphony. Like Dvořák, he com-
mitted himself to America. Dvořák's ambitions for
an "American school" of composers and for state-
supported American institutions of musical education
were also Seidl's ambitions. In Manhattan, Dvořák
and Seidl were inseparable colleagues and friends.

When it came time to celebrate the one hundredth
birthday of the *New World* Symphony in December
1993, I was the artistic advisor to the Brooklyn
Philharmonic Orchestra. The result was a festival
exploring the "American accent" of the music Dvořák
composed in New York and Iowa. Subsequently, as
the orchestra's executive director, I took the story of
Dvořák into Brooklyn middle- and high-school class-
rooms. For inner-city youngsters new to symphonic
music, Dvořák was a fascinating and heroic figure.
The students proved eager to identify with Dvořák's

search for an indigenous New World music distinguishable from Old World models. The music for our "Dvořák in America" programs in the Brooklyn schools typically included "Deep River" and "Goin' Home," Stephen Foster's "Old Folks at Home" in Dvořák's arrangement for chorus and orchestra, and excerpts from the *New World* Symphony, all with student performers and commentators taking part alongside professional players.

In 1999, I taught "Dvořák in America" at Boston's New England Conservatory. My students created lecture/recital programs featuring the *American* String Quartet, the *American Suite,* the Humoresques, and the Violin Sonatina. These became part of a three-week Dvořák unit at the Boston Latin School, where thirty twelfth graders were invited to ponder issues of race and culture as exposed by Dvořák's American sojourn—during which he was denounced in Boston as a "Negrophile." Whether sponsored by an orchestra or by a conservatory, "Dvořák in America" proved an ideal vehicle for introducing the symphonic experience while exploring the American experience. The fundamental questions Dvořák indefatigably asked—"What is America?" "Who is an American?"—are questions perpetually renewed and unfailingly rewarding.

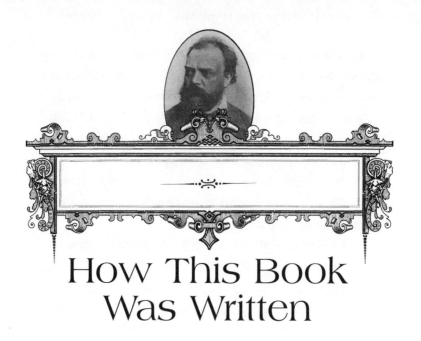

How This Book Was Written

Many readers will want to know how much of what I have written is demonstrably "true."

When a conductor performs a piece of music—say, the *New World* Symphony by Antonín Dvořák—he is expected to serve as an "interpreter." The composer, of course, has furnished a "score": notes on paper, plus various additional indications—how fast or slow, how loud or soft, where to get faster or louder, slower or softer. But it is understood, both by composer and performer, that this written blueprint is incomplete. The conductor is of course expected to obey the composer's instructions. But he or she is also expected to "read between the lines," to creatively convey the "spirit" of the piece, to imaginatively and empathetically "become" the composer. Writing about Dvořák in America, especially for young people, invites a comparable exercise. In my book, I have set forth the facts of Dvořák's American sojourn. But—in further pursuit of fidelity to the composer—I have also endeavored to imagine what it felt like to be Antonín Dvořák in Manhattan or in Spillville. My account, in this sense, is as true as I could make it.

It may be useful to contrast my method with that of Josef Skvorecky in his well-known *Dvořák in Love*. This splendid 1983 novel of Dvořák, Harry Burleigh, Jeannette Thurber, and James Gibbons Huneker begins with what is known. But Skvorecky's fiction is quite unconstrained. With a novelist's gift, he freely invents incidents and themes—including two ancillary love affairs, coupling Kovařík with Otilka Dvořák, and Jeannette Thurber's colleague Adele Margulies with Dvořák's African American student Will Marion Cook—to consummate a tale, necessarily speculative, centering on Dvořák's secret love for his sister-in-law. Most of the events I have more modestly imagined, by comparison, had to have taken place in some fashion. Although we don't know exactly what he saw, said, or felt, Dvořák necessarily glimpsed the Manhattan skyline for the first time. He had to have had an initial meeting with Burleigh. He could not have avoided discussing the *New World* Symphony with Anton Seidl. Where I show Dvořák pub hopping with Huneker, I embroider an incident recalled in Huneker's autobiography, *Steeplechase.* Where I have Burleigh eulogize Dvořák, I compose a speech we know Burleigh actually delivered in 1941 at Dvořák's former East Seventeenth Street residence.

Readers—especially young readers—interested in knowing more are directed, first, to Robert Winter and Peter Bogdanoff's DVD *From the New World: A Celebrated Composer in America,* created in tandem with this book. The DVD contains a wealth of primary sources, illustrations, and audio materials, many of which are referenced in these notes. (All pertinent DVD sections and documents are indexed on the DVD as *"Dvořák in America,* Reader's Links.")

Michael Beckerman's *New Worlds of Dvořák* (2003) is an indispensable study. *Dvořák and His World* (1993), edited by Beckerman, includes some fascinating American documents not elsewhere available. No longer in print, but worth a look, is *Dvořák in America* (1993), an anthology edited by John C. Tibbetts. *Dvořák and America* (2000), a sixty-minute television documentary concentrating on Dvořák and Burleigh, is available from PBS Home Video.

Much of the information in my Prelude, "Young Harry Burleigh," may be found in Jean Snyder's Burleigh essay in the Tibbetts anthology.

Chapter 1, "New York Greets Dvořák," re-creates Dvořák's arrival. That he docked first in Hoboken, that he was greeted by a Czech delegation and by Edmund Stanton, and that he found the Clarendon Hotel too expensive are historical facts. Henry Krehbiel's article "Antonín Dvořák" appeared in *Century* magazine, volume 44 (May–October 1892); the entire text may be found in Winter and Bogdanoff's DVD. The meeting with Thurber, Huneker, and James Creelman is my invention. The tour of "eating and drinking establishments" is described in volume 2 (pp. 65–69) of Huneker's *Steeplechase*. The words I have put in his mouth partly come from this and other Huneker writings. Victor Herbert's cameo appearance is an interpolation to facilitate a composers' discussion of American musical prospects. The letter ("Dear Sir, Esteemed Madam") is a conflation of three Dvořák letters: to Mr. and Mrs. Hlávka on November 27, 1892, to Dr. Emil Kozánek on October 12, 1892, and to Karel Battar on October 14, 1892 (see DVD).

Chapter 2, "Dvořák Gets His Bearings," begins with a "letter" based primarily on a passage from Kovařík's reminiscences, dealing with Central Park, locomotives, and steamships. (See DVD. I have obviously reformatted this text in the present tense.) Kovařik's memoirs may be found in Otakar Sourek's collection of Dvořák-related *Letters and Reminiscences*, as translated by Roberta Samsour (published in Prague in 1954). The visit to the opera is another passage from Kovařík's memoirs (see DVD). The vignette of Dvořák as teacher, grinding and grunting, is from the 1919 reminiscences of two Dvořák students (see DVD). For more on Dvořák at the National Conservatory, see Emanuel Rubin's essay in Tibbetts. The *Slavonic Dances* that made Dvořák's reputation may be sampled on the DVD. It seems that it was Huneker who introduced Burleigh to Dvořák, but nothing is known about what, precisely, happened next.

Chapter 3, "Buffalo Bill and *Hiawatha*," re-creates the Madison Square Garden Wild West show we know Dvořák saw with Thurber. An excellent resource is *Buffalo Bill and the Wild West,* a catalog published by the Brooklyn Museum (1981). Krehbiel's writings on Native American music may be found on the DVD. I also discuss Krehbiel's liberal attitudes toward music and race (he was no Social Darwinist) in my *Wagner Nights* (pp. 330–35). *The Song of Hiawatha* is readily available as an inexpensive Everyman paperback. On *Hiawatha* and the *New World* Symphony, see Beckerman's *New Worlds of Dvořák.*

Chapter 4, "Dvořák and the 'Yellow' Press," relies on Beckerman's ingenious discovery of Creelman's role in the Dvořák story. "Real Value of Negro Melodies" is an abridgment of the original article (see DVD). Dvořák wrote that the musician "must prick his ear for music" in *Harper's* magazine (see DVD). On yellow journalism, see Joyce Milton, *The Yellow Kids* (1989). For Creelman's campaign of letters and statements, see the DVD. Dvořák's April 12, 1893, letter to Kozánek is an abridgment (see DVD).

Chapter 5, "Spillville," treats a summer idyll many times described; especially vivid are the tape-recorded recollections of Czech Americans who knew Dvořák (see DVD). Tibbetts and Beckerman valuably consider the Spillville summer. I am indebted to John Mack Faragher of Yale University for his insights into the Kickapoo Medicine Show. Dvořák's letter is a conflation of letters to Kozánek on September 15, 1893, and to Anton Rus on August 17, 1893 (see DVD). All the pertinent music—the Violin Sonatina, the *American* Suite, the *American* Quartet—may be found on the DVD. My analysis of the Larghetto from the Sonatina is indebted to Beckerman's.

Chapter 6, "The *New World* Symphony," begins with an imagined conversation between Dvořák and the hero of my *Wagner Nights:* Anton Seidl, who indeed slowed down the second movement of the *New World* Symphony. For more on Seidl's remarkable Coney Island concerts, see *Wagner Nights,* pp. 199–212. For Krehbiel's long article in full (*New York Tribune,* December 17, 1893), see the DVD. The "American accent" of the *New World* Symphony has been extensively explored by Beckerman, also by Winter and myself (see DVD). Beckerman has also created a "*Hiawatha* Melodrama," superimposing verses from Longfellow's poem on parts of movements three and four of Dvořák's symphony. Winter's colleague Peter Bogdanoff has created a "visual presentation" for movements two and three of the *New World* Symphony, using passages from Longfellow and canvases by such Americans as Catlin, Remington, Bierstadt, and Audubon. I have had a hand in both these creations (and have presented both in concert). That the sadness of Dvořák's Largo resonates with the early deaths of three of his children is a personal inference. There are numerous eyewitness accounts of the premiere of the *New World* Symphony: of the audience breaking into applause midway through, of Seidl motioning to Dvořák, of the critics mobbing Dvořák's box (see DVD). Dvořák's comment to Creelman is also documented. For Henderson's review, see the DVD. Dvořák's reaction to Henderson is pure Horowitz.

Chapter 7, "A Tale of Two Cities," draws on my own extensive research into Boston versus New York (see my forthcoming *Classical Music in the United States: A History*). For responses to Dvořák from Chadwick, Beach, and other Boston musicians, and for various reviews, see the DVD. Krehbiel must have at least glimpsed Philip Hale at the Boston Symphony concert; I invented Krehbiel's rubbing of his tummy. On Agassiz and Social Darwinism, a vivid account is that of Louis Menand in *The Metaphysical Club* (2001). It is Beckerman's expert opinion that Creelman at least coauthored "Dvořák Leads for the Fund." For this article (*New York*

Herald, January 24, 1894), see the DVD. On the interpretation of "Old Folks at Home," see (for example) Ken Emerson's Stephen Foster biography, *Doo-dah!* (1997). Blackface racial stereotypes are of course unacceptable today. But contemporary scholarship more depicts Foster as a compassionate poet of displacement than as a thoughtless racist. On blackface minstrelsy, a useful starting point is Robert Toll's *Blacking Up* (1974). For Dvořák's "Music in America" (here greatly abridged), see the DVD.

For the Postlude, "Old Harry Burleigh," I reconstructed Burleigh's speech, partly relying on his own writings.

About the Author

Joseph Horowitz was born in New York City in 1948. He was a music critic for the *New York Times* from 1977 to 1980. His previous books are *Conversations with Arrau* (1982, winner of an ASCAP/Deems Taylor Award), *Understanding Toscanini: How He Became an American Culture-God and Helped Create a New Audience for Old Music* (1987), *The Ivory Trade* (1990), *Wagner Nights: An American History* (1994, winner of the Irving Lowens Award of the Society of American Music), and *The Post-Classical Predicament* (1995). From 1992 to 1997 he served as artistic advisor and then executive director of the Brooklyn Philharmonic Orchestra, resident orchestra of the Brooklyn Academy of Music, and there created educational outreach programs using the story of Dvořák in America. He has also served as an artistic advisor to other American orchestras, most regularly the New Jersey Symphony and the Pacific Symphony. He has taught at the Eastman School, the Institute for

Studies in American Music at Brooklyn College, the New England Conservatory, the Manhattan School of Music, and Mannes College. He regularly contributes articles and reviews to the Sunday *New York Times* and the *Times Literary Supplement* (UK). Other publications for which he has written include *American Music, The American Scholar, The Musical Quarterly, The New York Review of Books,* and *Nineteenth Century Music.* He lives in New York City with his wife Agnes and children Bernie and Maggie.

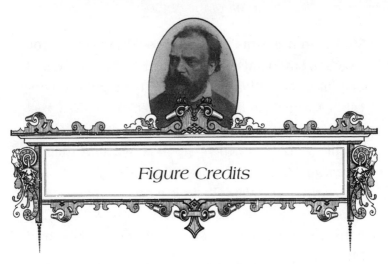

Figure Credits

P. iii: Antonín Dvořák . New York Philharmonic
Archives.

P. 2: Harry Burleigh with his brother and grandfather.
Courtesy of Jean Snyder and the Burleigh family.

P. 12: Antonín Dvořák. New York Philharmonic Archives.

P. 14 and cover: Manhattan. Collection of the New-York
Historical Society, George P. Hall Collection, negative number 75495.

P. 18: Union Square. Collection of the New-York
Historical Society, shows/crowds, negative number
75497.

P. 35: The aviary in the Central Park Zoo. Collection of
the New-York Historical Society, newspaper illustra-
tion, negative number 75498.

P. 40: Prague in 1885. Courtesy of Pavel Scheuflers.

P. 49: Young Harry Burleigh. Courtesy of Jean Snyder
and the Burleigh family.

P. 55: Buffalo Bill. Buffalo Bill Historical Center, Cody
WY; p.69.124.

P. 56: The Wild West show. Buffalo Bill Historical
Center, Cody WY; p.69.896.

Index

Agassiz, Louis, 121, 123
American Indians. *See* Native
    Americans
American Plantation Dances
    (Arnold), 48, 126
American String Quartet
    (Dvořák), 95–96,
    119–20, 134, 141
American Suite (Dvořák),
    94–95, 141
Anderson, Marian, 136
Arnold, Maurice, 48, 80, 102,
    126

Beach, Amy, 115
Beethoven, Ludwig van, 5, 48
Blackface minstrelsy, 9–10
Bohemia
    Czech communities in
        America, 37–38, 81,
        82–86
    Dvořák's birth and death,
        39, 133
    influence in *New World*

Symphony, 99–100, 107
    letters home to, 29–38,
        79–81, 89–92
    music in, 28, 42–43, 46
    nationalism, 43–44
    Slavs as cultural under-
        dogs, 39, 42, 46, 116,
        121–22
Boston, MA, *New World*
    Symphony in, 114–21,
    123
Boston Symphony Orchestra,
    48, 114, 116
Brahms, Johannes, 24, 104,
    105, 136, 138
"Buffalo Bill" Cody, **47,**
    54–59, 61
Burleigh, Harry, 1–10, **2,**
    48–53, **49,** 74, 99, 127,
    135–38, **136**

Carnegie Music Hall, New
    York, 101–10, **102,**
    103, 105

Carreño, Teresa, 5, 6, 7
Catlin, George, 59–61, **60,** 63
Cello Concerto (Dvořák), 134
Central Park Zoo, New York,
 34, **35**
Chicago, IL, 62, 85, 90–92
Cody, William F. "Buffalo
 Bill," **47,** 54–59, 61
Columbian Exhibition,
 Chicago, 62, 85, 90–92
Concerto for Violin in D major
 (Brahms), 104, **105**
Creelman, James
 Dvořák's introduction to,
  23, 47
 on *Herald's* Free Clothing
  Fund benefit, 124–25,
  126
 on premiere of *New World*
  Symphony, 102, 110,
  114
 and "yellow journalism,"
  73–78, **74,** 100
Cuba, in Spanish American
 War (1898), 75–76

"Deep River" (spiritual), 50,
 51, 79, 99, 136, 141
Dvořák, Anna, 12, 15, 17, **31,**
 83, 110
Dvořák children, 12, 13, 15,
 21, 26, **31,** 37, 80–81, 83,
 101, 106, 110

Fisher, William Arms, 133–34
Fleischmann's Restaurant,
 New York, 25, 47, 97

Foster, Stephen, 5, 9–10, 74,
 112, 127, 141

German culture as dominant,
 39, 42, 46, 47, 116,
 121–22
"Go Down, Moses" (spirit-
 ual), 3, 50

Hale, Thomas, 117
Hapsburg Empire, 39, 43, 47
Hearst, William Randolph,
 74, 76
Henderson, W. J., 110–12,
 120
Herbert, Victor, 25–26, 53, 98
Humoresques (Dvořák), 141
 in G-flat, 134
Huneker, James Gibbons,
 23–24, 28–29, 47, 48,
 78–79, 100, 144
Hungarian Rhapsody (Liszt), 6,
 44

"Indian Gallery" show
 (Catlin), **60**–61
Iowa, 37–38, 81, 82–96, **90,**
 91

Jones, Sissieretta "Black
 Patti," 126, 127
Joplin, Scott, 95
Joseffy, Rafael, 5, 7, 102

Kickapoo Medicine Show,
 85–88, **87**
Kovařík, Jan, 33, 81, 83, 85, 96

Kovařík, Josef, 13, 15, 22–23,
  33–**38,** 81, 83, 85, 96,
  137
Krehbiel, Henry Edward
  on American themes in
    New World Symphony,
    100–101
  article on Dvořák, 19–20
  criticism of "yellow jour-
    nalism," 78
  on Native American
    music, 61–63
  on Negro melodies, 47, 48,
    74, 115
  as "Negrophile," 120
  review of Boston perform-
    ance, 114, 115, 116–19

Longfellow, Henry
  Wadsworth, 28, 63–70,
  79, 106–10, 111

MacDowell, Edward, 21, 98
Madison Square Garden, New
  York, 55, 123, 124–29
Manhattan, Dvořák's views
  of, 13, **14–15,** 15–16,
  26, 27
Maple Leaf Rag (Joplin), 95
Minnehaha Falls, St. Paul, 93
Minstrelsy, blackface, 9–10

National Conservatory of
  Music, New York
  African Americans and, 7,
  8, 22, 52, 73

Burleigh and, 48–53
Creelman and, 77–78
Dvořák's exposure to, 47,
  48–53, 80
Herald's Free Clothing
  Fund benefit, 124–29
Seidl and, 25
Stanton and, 16, 22–23
Native Americans
  Catlin's portraits of,
    59–61, **60,** 63
  influence on *New World*
    Symphony, 111–13
  Kickapoo Medicine Show,
    85–88, **87**
  music of, 47, 61–63, 86, 88
  in *The Song of Hiawatha*
    (Longfellow), 28,
    63–70, 79, 93, 106–10,
    108–9, 111
Negro melodies
  Bostonians' views of,
    114–15, 118
  Burleigh's arrangements
    of, 136–37
  Creel's article on value of,
    71–73, 77
  Dvořák on, 132
  Dvořák's exposure to, 47,
    48–53, 80
  future of, 134–35
  and Native American
    music, 86, 88
  spirituals, 3, 25, 28–29,
    50–52, 79, 99, 104,
    111–12, 127, 132,

133–34, 135, 138
  reflected in *New World*
    Symphony, 133–34
"Negrophile," Dvořák
  denounced as, 120–21,
    141
Newspapers and "yellow
    journalism," 71–79
New World Symphony
    (Dvořák)
  Andante in, 98–99
  in Boston, 114–21, 123
  completion of, 79–80, 81
  Largo in, 98–99, 104, 105,
    133
  premiere of, 101–10, 112,
    140
  review of premiere,
    110–13
  Seidl and, 97–100
New York, Dvořák's views of,
  13, **14–15**, 16, **26, 27,
  102, 103, 105**. *See also*
  specific topics
New York Philharmonic, 37,
  48, 101, 117–18

Oakley, Annie, 57
"Old Folks at Home" (Foster),
  9–10, 88, 127–28, 141

Panic of 1893, 123–26, 129
Prague, 22, **31–33,** 45, 133

Remington, Frederic, **68–69,
  108–9**

Requiem (Dvořák), 116
Robeson, Paul, 136

Schoolcraft, Henry R., 59
Seidl, Anton
  Dvořák's enjoyment of, 37
  as Dvořák's friend, 47–48,
    97–100, **99,** 140
  Huneker on, 24–25
Siegfried (Wagner), 37
Simrock, Fritz, 45–46
Sitting Bull, 59, 76
Slavery, 1–4, 51, 112–13, 121
Slavonic Dances (Dvořák),
    44–45, 94
Smetana, Bedrich, 44
Social Darwinism, 121
The Song of Hiawatha
    (Longfellow), 28,
    63–70, **68–69,** 79, 93,
    106–10, **108–9,** 111
Spanish American War
    (1898), 75–76
Spillville, IA, 37–38, 81,
    82–96, **90, 91**
Spirituals, Negro, 3, 25,
    28–29, 50–52, 79, 99,
    104, 111–12, 127, 132,
    133–34, 135, 138
St. George's Episcopal
    Church, New York, 135
St. Wenceslaus Church
    (Spillville, IA), 82, **83,
    84,** 85
Stabat Mater (Rossini), 126
Stanton, Edmund, 16–18, 22

"Swing Low, Sweet Chariot" (spiritual), 79, 104, 138

Thurber, Francis Beattie, 21–23, 28, 47, 70, 102, 129
Thurber, Jeannette, 19, 21, 46, 48, 58, 73, 100, 102, 120, 124–25, 129, 135
Trains, 16–17, 34–36, 83, 95
Tristan und Isolde (Wagner), 24

Underground Railroad, 4
Union Square, New York, 17, **18**

United States government, 47–48, 75–76, 123

Violin Sonatina (Dvořák), 93–94, 141

Wagner, Richard, 24–25, 37
Waters, Hamilton (Burleigh's grandfather), 1–4, **2**, 5, 51–52
Wild West show, 54–59, **55, 56**, 61
Women in America, Seidl on, 98

"Yellow journalism," 71–79